THE TRIAL OF MARY TODD LINCOLN

The Trial of
Mary Todd Lincoln

by

JAMES A. RHODES

and

DEAN JAUCHIUS

THE BOBBS-MERRILL COMPANY, INC.
Publishers
INDIANAPOLIS • NEW YORK

COPYRIGHT © 1959 BY THE BOBBS-MERRILL COMPANY, INC.
PUBLISHED IN THE UNITED STATES OF AMERICA

The Library of Congress has cataloged
this publication as follows:

Rhodes, James A.
    The trial of Mary Todd Lincoln, by James A. Rhodes and
Dean Jauchius. [1st ed.] Indianapolis, Bobbs-Merrill [1959].
    200 p. 22 cm.
    Includes bibliography.

    1. Lincoln, Mary (Todd) 1818–1882—Fiction. I. Jauchius, Dean,
joint author. II. Title.
PZ4.R478Tr   813.5   59–7225 ‡
Library of Congress.

Counsel for the Defense

It is easy to think of Mary Todd Lincoln as one of the heavy burdens Abraham Lincoln bore without complaint. According to tradition, she was unpredictable, hysterical and unbalanced. Lincoln students in the main have accepted this estimate without fully examining the facts. Some, indeed, have done her the injustice of apologizing for her.

The authors undertook to find out whether history had treated her fairly. On the surface, the sanity hearing which declared her a lunatic was the most damaging count against her. In their investigation of this proceeding they discovered something wrong. She was no more eccentric than many around her. The authors' digging uncovered a strong odor of kangaroo court. The brazen injustice of this trial, the high-handed denial of her civil rights made a travesty of the verdict

5

and called for a broader re-examination. They found that during the years in the White House she had let herself appear in an unflattering light in order to shield and guard her husband. They came to hold an entirely new picture of this anguished woman.

The authors were convinced that Mary deserved her day in court, and had never had it. And certainly she deserved a more sincere and searching defense than she was ever given.

Neither in the mental hospital to which she was condemned, nor at any time previously, had she had any of the benefits of modern psychiatric treatment. She stood alone, unprotected. Because of her valiant struggle and because of her great love and devotion to her immortal husband and her sons, she deserves a better niche in our history than the one to which she has been consigned.

The legal and medical philosophy behind the "snake pit" laws which summarily "put her away" operates today. In large areas of the country many of these same laws are still in force.

These are our thoughts as we complete *The Trial of Mary Todd Lincoln.*

JAMES A. RHODES
DEAN JAUCHIUS

The Trial of Mary Todd Lincoln

Chapter 1

A LITTLE MORE than ten years after the death of her martyred husband, Mrs. Abraham Lincoln was placed under arrest, taken into custody under threat of violence, hailed summarily into a courtroom—before a jury already impaneled, sworn and waiting—tried, found insane, ordered confined in an institution and stripped of approximately $56,000 in cash and securities.

By nightfall of the following day, she sat alone in the gloom of a room with barred windows, branded by court order as "Mary Lincoln, Lunatic." And in the enforced solitude of that room, she could contemplate that she had been made the victim of an elaborately contrived and smoothly executed plot to put her away. She could ponder the fact that three of the men involved most prominently in that plotting had been intimate friends of her late husband. Indeed, two of them had maneuvered for him the Republican presidential nomination of 1860 and then prodded and pushed him down the political trail to the White House. Mary Todd Lincoln could think, too, that this scheme which they had planned so carefully against her had, to achieve its end, required denial of every constitutional and statutory right afforded the accused. And she could reflect, bitterly, that it had utilized as its primary instrument her eldest and only surviving son. It was cruel irony that through his eldest son, men who had been his best friends had managed to take away the freedom of the desolate and troubled widow of the man universally hailed as "The Great Emancipator."

It actually happened.

The place was Chicago, Illinois.

The day was Tuesday, May 19, 1875.

The first sound of it, for Mary Todd Lincoln, anguished widow, was a knock at the door of her room in the Chicago Grand Pacific Hotel.

The time was about 1:00 P.M. Here are the facts:

When Mary Lincoln opened that hotel-room door, three people greeted her. They were a delivery boy, Leonard T. Swett, a prominent Chicago lawyer who had helped secure the presidential nomination for Abraham Lincoln at the convention of 1860, and Samuel M. Turner, manager of the hotel.

The bundle boy delivered eight pairs of lace curtains which Mary Lincoln had purchased earlier in the day. He left immediately. Swett, who wrote later that Mary Lincoln seemed cheerful and glad to see him, entered the room followed by Sam Turner, and advised Mrs. Lincoln that she was under arrest. About that time, according to Swett, Turner left the room.

Mary Lincoln was ladylike but firm. The contention that she was insane was preposterous. She was abundantly able to care for herself. Where was her son Robert? Who claimed she was insane?

Swett told her that Robert was waiting for her at the courtroom. He advised her that it was her son who had filed the affidavit necessary to bring her to trial. He said Judge David Davis, conservator of her late husband's estate and the most prominent manipulator in Lincoln's behalf at the national convention of 1860, believed her crazy. So did John T. Stuart, mayor of Springfield and her cousin, he added. So did he, Swett, and so did five physicians. Swett produced letters from the physicians for Mary to see.

Mary Lincoln decided stubbornly that she would not go with Swett to the courtroom. Swett said she had no choice in the matter. She had two alternatives, though, as concerned how she was to be taken to court. She could either go peaceably with him, or be handcuffed and taken forcibly by two officers now waiting downstairs. Which would it be?

Mary Lincoln chose to resist with words alone. They were bitter, sarcastic words. She denounced Swett and Judge Davis and Robert. She accused them of having mercenary motives. And yet, Swett testifies, she was ever the lady, never stooping to use of common words or phrases.

When she had finished, Swett insisted again, and he was rocklike and unyielding. It was a court order. She must go with him or the officers. There was no escape.

Mary Lincoln wept then. She threw up her hands and prayed, and called upon Abraham to release her and drive Swett away. And then she gave in.

Swett testifies that he refused to leave the room so that she might change her clothing. He told Mary, he says, that he feared she might commit suicide. And so the resigned Mary Lincoln, erstwhile first lady of the land, stepped into a closet, made the desired changes and went along quietly.

The carriage took Mary Lincoln and her custodian to the criminal court and county jail building at West Hubbard and North Dearborn streets. A second carriage, bearing the two officers, Turner and Ben Ayer, serving with Swett as counsel for Robert Lincoln, followed them.

It must have been nearly 3:00 P.M. when the party arrived at the courtroom. Swett says that Mary argued with him in her room "from twenty minutes past one until half past two."

At any rate, a jury composed of twelve prominent Chicago business and professional men, most of them friends of Robert, had been impaneled, sworn and waiting since two o'clock. The courtroom was filling slowly with spectators. The increasing flow of them measured the speed with which word of the nature of this proceeding was flashing throughout the building.

Swett says that, when he opened the courtroom door and Mary Lincoln saw the men inside, she recoiled, and he urged her to come right along, saying that Robert was there and that he would sit beside her. Thus assured, Mary Lincoln entered quietly and sat down without speaking.

Swett went immediately to Robert, told him how his mother had denounced him at the hotel and testifies that he said: "We must act as though we were her friends and come sit beside her and do everything as though she was sane."

Robert walked to his mother, and she received him kindly. Swett says he told Mrs. Lincoln that she was entitled to counsel, that Isaac N. Arnold, her old friend, was present, and that "he was your husband's friend and maybe you would rather have him and Robert sit beside you than have a stranger brought in here."

Mary Lincoln agreed and Swett soon had Arnold sitting with her.

Swett says he then went to Ben Ayer and advised his colleague that the experience with Mrs. Lincoln had tired him. He urged Ayer to take over.

But as they were conversing, Arnold, who had conferred briefly with Mary Lincoln, approached them and expressed doubt about the propriety of defending Mary. He expressed a belief that she was insane.

"This means," Swett says he retorted, "that you will put into her head that she can get some mischievous lawyer to make us trouble; go and defend her, and do your duty."

The well-oiled courtroom machinery, waiting and ready since 2:00 P.M., got into motion immediately after this exchange. On the bench was Judge M. R. M. Wallace, a Democrat and known political enemy of the late President Lincoln. He observed that the trial was a hearing on an application to try the question of the sanity of Mrs. Lincoln, and to appoint a conservator for her estate. Robert Lincoln's petition, he told the jury, represented to the court that Mary Lincoln, widow of Abraham Lincoln, deceased, and a resident of Cook County, was insane, and that for her benefit and for the safety of the community she should be confined.

The petition also prayed that a conservator be

appointed to manage and control Mary Lincoln's estate, and estimated it to be valued "not exceeding $75,000."

Robert Todd Lincoln's position was that he should be named conservator. Judge Davis, handling his late father's estate, was much too busy, he contended.

Specifically, then, Robert Lincoln wanted the court to do two things: 1. Send his mother to an asylum. 2. Permit him to take over her estate.

To support his contention that his mother was a lunatic, Robert Lincoln had summoned seventeen witnesses. With at least some of these witnesses, the testimony they were to give had been carefully gone over. There is reason to believe that all of the witnesses had been present at pretrial conferences.

By way of contrast, Mary Lincoln, the accused, had not even been given time to select her own defense attorney. One had conveniently been provided for her. She had been given no opportunity to summon friendly witnesses and no time to prepare a defense against a charge and testimony to support it which had been carefully assembled over a three-week period. She had been denied the statutory right of participating in the selection of the jury of her peers through interrogation of prospective jurors and the exercising of peremptory challenges which might be deemed to be in her best interests.

In short, she was being railroaded in a courtroom pungent with a kangaroo odor and manned by a jury having about it the air of one impaneled to convict.

In the next three hours a parade of seventeen witnesses piled up a mountain of damaging testimony, loaded with hearsay and with conclusions by those testifying. And this testimony was neither challenged nor examined by a meek little defense attorney famed for representing and obtaining acquittals for women in trouble with the law. The right of cross-examination was not invoked.

Ayer had conducted the case for the plaintiff so far. Now that the final witness, Robert Todd Lincoln himself, had finished, Swett took over again. He presented the final argument for the plaintiff to the jury, saying that it was too bad about Mary Lincoln but she was plainly deranged and must be put away. And so the man who had first urged Robert to take this action, and who then had served as Mary Lincoln's arresting officer and custodian, now assumed the role of prosecutor. He called for a quick verdict and got it. The jurors deliberated for perhaps a full two minutes and found Mary Lincoln insane. The specific wording of the verdict which they managed to prepare and sign in that brief space of time was:

"We the undersigned, jurors in the case of Mary Lincoln who is alleged to be insane, having heard the

evidence adduced, are satisfied that the said Mary
Lincoln is insane, and is a fit person to be sent to the
State Hospital for the Insane: that she is a resident
of the County of Cook, in the State of Illinois: that
her age is 56 years; that her disease is of unknown
duration; that the cause is unknown; that the disease
is not with her hereditary; that she is not subject to
epilepsy: that she does not manifest homicidal or suicidal tendencies and that she is not a pauper."

It was nearly a month before the court got around
to answering the second prayer in Robert Lincoln's
petition by appointing him conservator of his mother's
estate. But the court's first decision was quite prompt.
Judge Wallace immediately ruled:

"Whereupon, upon the verdict aforesaid, it is considered and adjudged by the Court that the said Mary
Lincoln is an insane person, and it is ordered that said
Mary Lincoln be committed to a State Hospital for
the Insane, and it is further ordered that a summons
be issued to the said Mary Lincoln commanding her to
appear before this Court and show cause if any she
has or can show why a conservator should not be
appointed to manage and control her estate."

In less than five hours—one hour and ten minutes
of this time consumed by Mary's argument with
Swett in her hotel room—Abraham Lincoln's widow
had been arrested, tried, found guilty and ordered im-

prisoned. Now it remained for her to be relieved of her wealth. Swett, instigator, architect, arresting officer, custodian and prosecutor, now took it on himself to perform this final chore.

From the moment of her entry into the courtroom, Swett testifies, "she never spoke." Now, she sought to evade this final surrender of what she called "these bonds I have saved for my necessities in my old age." Swett threatened force again. He pointed out that he could get an order of writ or have the sheriff take them forcibly from her. He asked her to turn them over to Robert.

Mary refused. Robert, she said, could never have anything that belonged to her.

Swett suggested that she turn the securities over to Arnold. Mary suggested that it be done in her hotel room. "It is so hot here."

At her room in the Grand Pacific they took them from her, and Swett says of the act, "and when she did yield, although she yielded peaceably, she yielded as to force."

Swett arranged for her care during the night and left. Newspapers were informed the following morning that Mary Todd Lincoln had made an unsuccessful attempt to poison herself. They printed the story.

Mary Lincoln was not sent to the State Hospital

for the Insane, as was suggested by the jury's verdict. Instead, she was taken to Bellevue Place Sanatorium, a private institution owned and operated by Dr. R. J. Patterson at Batavia, Illinois.

This first sanity trial of Mary Todd Lincoln has remained among the more obscure episodes in American history. Historians have been loath to illuminate it. Lincoln students have tended to avoid careful scrutiny of it.

But if they have given this first trial short notice, they have given the second one even less attention. It, too, had the same peculiar flavor as the first. It lasted less than four minutes. Mary Lincoln was found restored to reason and given her freedom. Her lawyer was Leonard Swett!

There are probably many valid reasons why historians have given such scant attention to this peculiar and coldly brutal treatment of Lincoln's aging widow. Certainly, one of them is that the transcript of the trial has long since disappeared. The exact circumstances of its disappearance are not known. It is known that the son who was used as the instrument for bringing his mother to trial and subsequent incarceration in an asylum expressed intent to do away with certain records pertaining to the action.

But if the disappearance of these papers is a valid reason for failure to illuminate the trial or trials, it also is a stimulant to one's curiosity.

Mary Todd Lincoln regarded the entire episode as simply a plot to get her money, and she said so. However, in the light of subsequent events, this explanation reeks too much of the easy answer. Her release was managed within one year and one month by the very man who first suggested the plan to put her away. Her money was returned to her, along with a scrupulous accounting by her son.

Historians have tended to regard the episode of the first trial as a painful incident in the life of a tragic figure who had suffered such blows that they deranged her. But Mary Lincoln continued to exhibit, after regaining her freedom, those same eccentricities which were used to convince a jury of her derangement.

Granted that Mary Lincoln possessed more than the usual number of eccentricities, it is not to be assumed that she was possessed by them. Indeed, many of them are quite understandable and are manifested today in many, many persons whose sanity goes unchallenged.

In Mary Lincoln, much more so than in most people, the eccentricities are understandable. Her search for love and understanding after the death of her husband and three of her four children seemed a futile one. She turned for friendship to the clerks in stores which she patronized. It is an understatement to remark that there was a "misunderstanding" between Mary Todd Lincoln, the lonely widow, and Mary Harlan Lincoln, Robert's wife. The feeling was sufficiently strong to prevent Robert's mother from visiting his home in Chicago.

Abraham Lincoln had been dead for ten years at the time of Mary's first trial, and yet the hatreds and the malevolence unleashed by the angry controversy which had him at its storm center still seethed across the land. Even the great financial panic which had gripped the country since 1873 could not deter those men who were dedicated to seeking out strange vengeances against Lincoln's memory.

But Lincoln had the martyr's cloak across his memory now, and he was becoming immortal. His name already had risen to such giant proportions that his memory would prove unassailable. Nothing could damage it. Certainly, the spectacle of a little old lady who was his widow sometimes acting strangely could not hurt it. Indeed, this could only serve to emphasize the extent of the tragedy which had fallen on her and on the nation.

If Leonard Swett, Isaac N. Arnold and Judge David Davis had been such close friends of Abraham Lincoln, why would they now turn on his helpless widow and railroad her into an asylum? And why would her own son permit himself to be a part of it? Would not that do more damage than service to Lincoln's memory?

None of these three men had changed in their attitudes toward Lincoln. They defended his good name with eloquent ferocity when it came under attack after his assassination.

Indeed, the very existence of such stark contrast between Lincoln's known somber honesty and outspoken integrity and the conditions brought on by spoilers and looters in power ten years later is what suggests a much deeper and more basic political motive for the day of infamy in Mary Lincoln's life.

While Lincoln lived, Springfield and Chicago had become the political capitals of the nation. Illinois men ruled the political roost. Now, since his death, and owing to the flow of favors from the fountainhead of power in the White House, the geographical center of political power was shifting eastward into Ohio, even as the center of population shifted westward to the Buckeye State. The spoils system, and excesses in Washington, had brought men honestly devoted to Lincoln and his integrity up short. A grave split ripped through the new Republican Party. Stanch supporters of U. S. Grant, or of what Grant stood for, became known as Stalwarts. The reformist wing was composed of men who became known as Liberal Republicans, sometimes called half breeds by the Stalwarts.

Judge David Davis, the old manipulator who traded his way to the nomination of Abraham Lincoln in 1860, turned furiously on the men whom he believed to be destroying his party's integrity. In 1872 he secured nomination as the National Labor Party's candidate for President and sought nomination by the Liberal Republican Party at that convention in Cincinnati in June. There is strong suspicion that he intended to obtain endorsement of his candidacy by the Democratic National Convention and by the Liberal Colored Republican Convention. But the Liberal Republican Convention stopped him cold, nominating Horace Greeley, distinguished editor of the New York *Tribune,* instead. Greeley went on to win the Democratic National Convention nod and the approval of the Liberal Colored Republicans only to lose to the popular Hero of Appomattox in the fall election.

If Grant had overcome the liberal wing, however, he had not overcome the resentment of its members. As 1876—the next convention and election year—approached, Grant began to speak of a third term. There was too much objecting in the press, however, and the Stalwarts began to cast about for a successor.

Robert Todd Lincoln, a stalwart Stalwart who gave

unstintingly of his loyalty to the Grant crowd, was yet too much of a sapling for presidential timber, but the name was political magic. It could be used. And, perhaps four or eight years hence, it would be the name which would be used to keep the Stalwarts in the White House.

Judge Davis, veteran politician, could hardly miss this. Neither could Leonard Swett nor Isaac N. Arnold.

Robert Lincoln said he regarded Judge David Davis as a second father. There is evidence that Davis had a similar, reciprocal affection for Robert. But no affection, not even devotion to Abraham Lincoln, ever swayed Davis from resorting to manipulations to achieve victory in a political fight, and now Davis, an independent turning Democrat, was in a political fight.

How to damage Robert Lincoln to prevent him from enjoying a political sleigh ride, or providing one for the spoilers, on his father's name? How to do it and yet leave the sacred memory of Abraham Lincoln stainless?

It makes sense that they found their way to eliminate Robert Lincoln as a serious political factor in the drumhead sanity hearing on May 19 and its aftermath. They advised Robert Lincoln to push for his mother's commitment; they helped him make the arrangements and collect his witnesses. Swett made the arrest, helped prosecute the case. Arnold was appointed to defend Mary Lincoln. After a request for postponement was denied, he did almost nothing in her behalf. The hearing swept through unchallenged to the jury's verdict, which came so fast that it may have been written out in advance of the trial.

Thus Robert Lincoln became the man who committed his mother to the insane asylum. Mary Lincoln's letters made it clear to many of her friends that she believed he did it to get hold of her money. Before long she interested Judge and Mrs. James Bradwell in her case. These respected and influential people likewise spread the word that she had been wronged by her only surviving son.

After a few months she was "paroled" from the mental hospital to her sister's home in Springfield. Evidently she was not very crazy.

On June 15, 1876, James G. Blaine, a Grant Stalwart, was beaten in a strong bid to obtain the presidential nomination. Governor Rutherford B. Hayes of Ohio, a man of reformist sentiments, wrested the nomination away from Colonel Robert G. Ingersoll's "plumed knight" on the seventh ballot, and the reign of the spoilers was apparently over.

And later in that same day, June 15, Mary Todd Lincoln was adjudged sane and her property restored to her control in a proceeding which occupied, according to the Chicago *Tribune* of the following day, "but a few minutes." The timing is suggestive. During the intervening thirteen months, the name of Robert Lincoln had been so hammered by an enraged mother and by her allies, the Bradwells, that it could well have suffered the most devastating political damage.

The second sanity hearing, which declared Mary Todd Lincoln of sound mind and capable of handling her own property, must have been as well arranged as the first. It lasted less than five minutes. Leonard Swett this time was on the other side of the fence and represented her. There was no opposition.

Neither Robert Todd Lincoln nor his name ever became a major force in national politics after his participation in the sanity proceedings against his mother. His last political gasp left him standing at the depot in Chicago in 1880 looking after the presidential band wagon as it pulled out. He had ridden through thirty-six convention ballots with Grant, only to see his hero finally fall before the late sprint of a dark horse named James A. Garfield.

Robert Todd Lincoln became Garfield's secretary of war, an appointment which clearly represented a concession to the Stalwarts. He was the only member of the official family to be retained by President Arthur, the Stalwart Vice President who ascended to the White House after Garfield's death from bullet wounds inflicted by an assassin. And Arthur's retention of Lincoln underscored the fact that the son of the Great Emancipator was the only Garfield cabinet member fully acceptable to Grant admirers.

The name of Robert Lincoln was mentioned vaguely here and there in 1881 and 1882 as a presidential possibility for 1884, but there seems to have been some stigma attached to his name by then. There is ample reason to identify it as the fact that he had sent his anguished mother to a lunatic asylum.

In this nation which her husband had so eloquently characterized as "dedicated to the proposition that all men are created equal," the most humble person was entitled to a fair trial and to a virile defense, and yet Mary Lincoln was given no real trial at all and only a passive, yielding defense. Presented in the trial episode which follows is the kind of defense to which she was entitled, even if she had been a nobody, let alone the widow of the Great Emancipator. Presented are questions which ought to have been put to witnesses who appeared against her, and the answers which those witnesses would have been required to give to avoid perjury.

The outcome of that infamous first trial can never

be changed, but with the use of known facts, it is possible to uncover the motive which demanded the verdict so quickly rendered.

In a larger sense, the trial of Mary Lincoln was much more than her first trying ordeal in that Chicago courtroom in 1875 or her second brief encounter with a most peculiar brand of justice in 1876 only hours after the Stalwarts had been beaten in their bid to retain a firm grip on the White House. These were but small persecutions in a much longer trial which commenced for her on the somber morning of April 15, 1865, when Abraham Lincoln drew his last breath.

Mary Todd Lincoln passed away July 16, 1882, at Springfield, Illinois, after lapsing into a coma which modern men of medicine generally believe to have been diabetic. Death came to her in a cheerful room of the house in which she and Abraham had become man and wife.

The trial of Mary Todd Lincoln, therefore, did not span a few infamous hours. It lasted for seventeen years and three months, and the verdict of history is that she was innocent.

Chapter 2

WITHOUT THE HELP, as well as the encouragement, of Judge Davis, Leonard Swett and Isaac Arnold, it seems unlikely that Robert Lincoln could so easily have had his mother committed to a lunatic asylum. He had collected seventeen witnesses, including amenable doctors who had not examined her, store clerks who thought her a little odd and private detectives whom he had had following her "to protect her," but he didn't have a strong case.

Isaac Arnold, who was appointed to represent Mrs. Lincoln, was ordinarily an aggressive and capable lawyer. On May 19 he was unaccountably meek. He did not protest against the jury's having been selected and sworn before Mrs. Lincoln arrived at court and without challenge from the defense. He had not investigated the witnesses and checked their evidence.

He did not cross-examine them and seek to invalidate their testimony. In fact, he hardly opened his mouth.

Without a strong and energetic defense Mrs. Lincoln had no chance before a judge and jury ready to rule against her.

Isaac Arnold, through inability or disinclination, did not work up a defense. But even at this distance, with many records destroyed, some no doubt indirectly or directly by Robert Lincoln, it is still possible to do what Isaac Arnold did not do—shred the case presented by the attorneys and witnesses in behalf of Mary Todd Lincoln's insanity. That case has now been prepared. The jury has been investigated. The witnesses have been checked and their testimony evaluated.

Even in a hostile court a strong defense would have scored damaging point after damaging point. Very likely, with the judge and jury she faced, Mrs. Lincoln would still have been judged insane, but the verdict would have been in spite of, not in accord with, the facts presented.

The next few chapters will present the events of May 19, 1875, again but with one difference. Instead of an Isaac Arnold tacitly consenting to his client's commitment to a lunatic asylum, she will be represented by a vigorous lawyer with a well-prepared defense. Call him Isaac Arnold, the Isaac Arnold who was ordinarily an aggressive bulldog of a lawyer, a hard fighter for his clients. In challenging the jury, in cross-examining witnesses, he will make use of facts that were available at the time and are available still, facts that have been verified before they were allowed to appear here.

To repeat, the trial as it will be told in the following chapters never happened. It could have happened, and in justice it should have happened. Was the reason it did not a conspiracy on the part of Lincoln's old friends to prevent his son from siding with the spoilers in Washington and tearing down his father's work? You are the jury. Follow the case and decide.

Mary Lincoln consulted her chatelaine watch with sober, bluish-gray eyes and felt faintly startled. A quarter after eleven!

Goodness! she thought. I must hurry about this. There is so little time.

She cast a casual glance over her shoulder, as if it were meant only to take in the pleasant May day in Chicago. The man was still there. He always seemed to be there. Why did men follow her? Would they never stop? Did they want to harm her?

Mary Lincoln did not know, but the old fear drove through her and hurried her stride. Perhaps she ought to have remained in the hotel room, but there was something about a hotel room which always depressed her. She had been glad to get out of it. Besides, it was such a pleasant day, although the streets were still muddy from recent rains. She did not look, but she told herself that the dust ruffle of her black suit dress must be terribly smudged with mud.

It was all right, she told herself. She had found a friend, and today she would present that friend with a token of her esteem. A chatelaine watch similar to the one she wore. The girl named Beatrice had admired it so.

She turned her mind back to the hotel room. It was the small window that bothered her most, she decided. It formed a perfect frame for the chimney on the building next door. It was a chimney which constantly gave off black smoke, and this reminded her of the great Chicago fire. She wouldn't be at all surprised, she thought, if Chicago were to burn again. It was rickety, really, behind its façaded splendor.

Mary Lincoln could remember the great fire very clearly. It had come in that somber October after Tad's death at the Clifton House in July. That was why she had not gone back to the Clifton House upon her return to Chicago. She thought now of Tad. Kind, sweet, loving Tad.

The old anguish shot through her. She was not superstitious, but she told herself that somehow she would always regard the great Chicago fire of 1871 as a sort of omen. Tad, she reflected, had been the last of her sons who loved her, and after his passing, her life had lain about her in ashes, as the great Chicago business district was reduced to ashes.

Robert did not love her. Not really. She could see it in his eyes. Robert was cold, and he mixed with people who hated her. She sighed, wondering why people hated her so. Why?

Robert, she thought with an expression of distaste, was a Grant man. Mary Lincoln had never liked General Grant. Now she was indignant at what he was doing. Her generous mouth set itself firmly. Abraham would never have permitted such goings on. She told herself grimly that she would have seen to that.

She turned her mind back to Tad. In some ways, it seemed only yesterday that he had gasped his last in the room filled with pain and anguish at the Clifton House. And in others, it seemed so much longer than four years ago. Here it was May 19, 1875. How time does fly! She had been at the Grand Pacific Hotel now for two months. Two months ago last Saturday.

Mary halted uncertainly before the embossed façade of Matson and Company. She felt her bonnet, perched securely on her rich brown hair. This was the store where she had seen and ordered the watch.

She entered, her kid-gloved hands at the mourning brooch beneath her cape; she could visualize the picture of Abraham on it now.

"May I help you, madame?"

She had not seen the clerk approach. He had come up behind her. His voice startled her. She turned to face him. He knew her, of course. He was studying her intently. There was a strangeness in his eyes.

"I have come for the watch," she said simply. "The one I admired yesterday. Do you have it wrapped?"

The clerk said yes, he did have. He had had it gift-wrapped as she wanted. Was there anything else?

That would be all for now, she said.

"Will you take it with you, madame, or shall I have it delivered?" The clerk looked embarrassed.

Mary said she would take it with her. She was thinking that she would have no more of this delivery business. Somehow, Robert always seemed to find out, and he would have her purchases returned.

The clerk handed the watch to her, and she saw that the strangeness remained in his eyes. It made her uncomfortable. She moved quickly through the doorway and into the warm May sunshine again. Once she looked back. The man was still following. Splinters of apprehension raced through her. Did he mean her harm? Was he some crank? One of Abraham's

enemies, perhaps? Abraham had had so many enemies and they would not leave him alone. Not even
now.

Mary Lincoln shrugged imperceptibly. What did
it matter, really? They could never harm Abraham's
name now. He had been too big for them, a giant
among men. She managed a mysterious little smile,
which came to her sober eyes and mouth in her
smooth, round, unwrinkled face, and then left
abruptly.

She found the walk to the Charles Gossage and Company store most invigorating. Weariness had edged
her mind that morning for she had been quite unable
to sleep last night. Men kept following her. They
even followed her into the hotel. She reflected grimly
that Sam Turner, the manager, didn't believe her.
Neither did Mrs. Allen, the housekeeper at the hotel,'
nor Maggie Gavin, the maid. They just didn't understand her.

Was it unnatural to walk the floor when one
couldn't sleep? Mary Lincoln thought not. She had
done that as long as she could remember. So had
Abraham, when he lived. Often, late at night, she had
found him walking the floor at the White House.

There were a number of people abroad for such an
awkward hour of the morning. Some of them seemed

to know her, and nodded. She nodded back. The gentlemen tipped their hats. She thought that the ladies' eyes seemed curious.

She found Beatrice at the curtain counter, where she always was. Mary Lincoln liked Beatrice very much. She was a charming, lively-faced, merry-eyed young woman. And such manners! She had fine manners for a salesperson. Mary reflected that most salespersons she had known were inclined either to be abrupt or obsequious to the point of being nauseating. Beatrice was simply and genuinely affectionate. Sometimes, Mary Lincoln told herself, it was as though Beatrice were her daughter. She felt the old grief run through her then. She had always wanted a daughter. Could she have had a daughter, she reflected, she would have liked her to be like Beatrice.

Beatrice greeted her warmly. "My dear Mrs. Lincoln! How nice to see you again! Isn't it a lovely day? There is something about May days, I always say. A fine day for a little stroll." A pleasant smile was on Beatrice's lovely face. "You look very well, Mrs. Lincoln. Are you sleeping better now?"

Mary Lincoln said yes, she was, thank you, thinking that a little white lie was understandable here. No use to trouble such a sweet child. "My dear young lady! You yourself look tired. Are you working so terribly hard these days?"

Beatrice said wryly not as hard as she'd like. It was the depression. Wasn't it terrible, though? So many people out of work. "Not many people come here to purchase fine lace curtains such as these now. I do hope they will keep me on here. The good Lord knows it is little enough salary I draw as it is. They seem to dislike women clerks, you see."

Mary Lincoln removed her kid gloves and extended one small hand to feel the curtains. They were very fine curtains. Very fine indeed. There had never been better ones than this in the White House.

"They are lovely, my dear. I suppose you do have little call for them, though, since the panic."

"Almost none at all." Beatrice sighed. "People are most reluctant to buy."

"I shall take eight pairs of them," Mary Lincoln decided.

Beatrice's blue eyes showed her surprise. Then she blushed. "Oh, you needn't, really, ma'am. I did not mean it that way at all. I did not mean that you should buy some. . . ."

"It is all right, my dear. I shall need them one day, perhaps. Have them delivered to my room at the Grand Pacific."

"But . . ."

"No buts now, young lady. You have been very kind to me."

"Very well, Mrs. Lincoln. I'll have a bundle boy bring them around." She hesitated. "Will it be the usual charge?"

"No," Mary Lincoln decided. "No, I shall pay for them. I have some money today, you see. I have cashed one of my bonds."

Beatrice's eyes were on the chatelaine watch now. It gleamed expensively against the somber black of Mary Lincoln's clothing.

"It is such a pretty watch," Beatrice said. "I have always admired it."

"I know," Mary said. "It gave me a thought, my dear." She hesitated, then lifted the small, gift-wrapped box and placed it before her on the counter. "May I present you with a token of my esteem, my dear young lady? You have been so kind and friendly to me."

"Oh, Mrs. Lincoln. You shouldn't do these things! Only last week it was the perfume. Such expensive perfume, Mrs. Lincoln!" Beatrice's eyes were stabbing curiously at the package.

"Please," Mary Lincoln said. "You are a friend, dear young lady. Friends are such a blessing. I have so few real friends, you see."

Beatrice lifted the box carefully and then her slender fingers were working eagerly at its wrappings. At last, she had it open and she turned wide blue eyes to Mary.

"How lovely!"

Mary Lincoln could see the tears starting. "Please, child. Don't weep. It is as if you were a daughter, you see. I have always wanted a daughter. Abraham did, too." Mary Lincoln paused. "Dear, kind Abraham. How he would have spoiled a daughter!"

"But I just couldn't, Mrs. Lincoln. I mean, we are not supposed to accept gifts."

"Not accept gifts?" Mary Lincoln's smooth face grew stern. "Who says you are not allowed to accept gifts? Not allowed to accept offerings from the heart? My dear young lady, you will keep this watch." A plaintive note crept into her voice. She could not keep it out. "Keep it and remember me as a friend."

"Oh, Mrs. Lincoln." Beatrice was suddenly around the counter and embracing her. "Mother Lincoln. Who can say anything about you? You are so kind and good."

"There, there, my dear." Mary Lincoln felt a mother's tenderness surge through her. This was a sweet child. "There, there. Abraham and I have many enemies, you see. I think sometimes that even the worst of these do not know truly what it is they do."

Mary had quieted the sobbing girl. Now she turned slowly. She must go. She looked at her own watch again. After noon! She must hurry. The thought of lunch was not palatable to her. Neither was the thought of returning to her room. But she must go. She looked for the strange man. He was not there now. She turned back to Beatrice.

"There will be a man here inquiring about me soon," she said. "Do not tell him that I have purchased anything. They do not understand, you see, what my true need for such things is. No, do not tell him about this purchase and do not tell him where I am going. Why won't they leave me alone? Why do they follow me? What do they mean to do?"

"You look strange, Mrs. Lincoln. Out of your eyes, I mean. Is there something wrong?" Beatrice's yet moist blue eyes were filled with anxiety now.

"No." Mary Lincoln sighed. "No, nothing is wrong. My enemies are about me, you see, ready to strike again and again at my husband's memory through me. I suppose, my dear child, that they think that I do not know this. They close in upon me these days." Her generous mouth was set firmly. "But I shall triumph in the end. Mark my words, my child. I shall triumph."

The walk back to the hotel was very pleasant. She

was glad, now, that she had not taken the carriage. The street banks were steep, anyway, and made it very awkward for a lady. She felt better, too, for having given Beatrice the watch. It made her feel so good to do such things for her friends. Of all of the things in the world, Mary Todd Lincoln told herself, the greatest was to be surrounded by good friends. She knew why it was she felt this way. Love and affection had been ripped abruptly from her life. A woman needs love and affection, she thought. A woman needs them desperately.

The doorman at the Grand Pacific bowed, as always, but she detected a strangeness in his eyes, too. The elevator operator watched her slyly, and she wished she had not become so frightened the other night. To think of it now embarrassed her. Imagine running to the elevator in one's night clothing like a frightened child with a fever! She told herself she would not do that again, regardless of how frightened she might become.

There was something almost desolate about the room, in spite of its sumptuous furnishings. It seemed to close in on her as she entered. She stared at the small window, watching the black smoke belch from the chimney beyond it. Again she thought of Tad.

Poor Tad! It was terrible the way the boys back in Springfield used to tease him. Tongue-tied Tad they had called him.

That was why she had taken him to Europe. She wanted to get him away from them. He was such a bright child. It had helped, too. His diction had improved tremendously. And then—the trip home. She ought not to have come home, really. She had told herself that at the time, but she was ill and her spirits were low. The sea had been very rough. Heavy seas, the captain had called them. It was during the trip that Tad had taken the cold which brought his death. Mary Lincoln felt the tears coming and pressed them back. She took off her bonnet and cape, and then moved to the picture of her husband. She picked it up.

"Dear Abraham. They have said so many evil things about you, my dear," she said softly. "So many evil things. Men who pretended to be your friends. Men such as Herndon. How lonely are these years now that Tad, too, is gone! All of you have gone. Eddie, Willie, you, Tad. Love has gone, leaving only bitter ashes. Our enemies flourish, Abraham. They have made a mockery of the truth and of those things which you would have done. Were it not for this anger at them which stirs within me, I might have had done with it long ago. You must forgive me for this, Abraham. I have not your strength of character, you see—your great compassion. They wrong us and I want to forgive them, but I cannot. These are bitter, bitter days for the Lincoln name."

Mary Lincoln rose, setting the picture down, and strode to a window. Then she turned back to the picture, twisting off the wedding band on her finger to study the words engraved inside. They were still faintly legible. "Love is eternal," she muttered, raising sober blue-gray eyes again to the picture.

"Ah, Abraham, but that was sweet. Love is eternal? Yes, I think it is. It stays with me these trying years as nothing else. I feel it, sometimes, when I am troubled and when I am not quite myself. You were so gentle for such a big man and to think they said that you were awkward! Is there awkwardness in the grace of such love as ours? O Lord, help me to stand his absence until that time when I may be with him again. Give me his strength to stand these things they say. Give me his wisdom to deal with villainy."

Mary Lincoln stirred then and moved to her favorite chair. She must have some lunch. They had told her to eat regularly. She did not feel hunger now. Weariness assailed her. Why was it, she wondered, that her face did not betray this great weariness? She rose and walked to the mirror. Her rich brown hair remained fine and unfaded. There were no lines on her smooth face. In the eyes, perhaps, there was a kind of anguish. Nothing more. She sighed and returned to the chair.

Drowsiness assailed her. She dozed. Eddie was speaking to her now. Dear little Eddie. Only four. They had told her it was diphtheria. He was strangling, explaining to her in their Springfield home why it was that his tall, somber father was not with him at this hour.

"Papa don to tapila," he was saying. Papa gone to the capital. Congressman Lincoln was, indeed, in Washington. And a son was dying in Springfield.

The explosion startled her and she made a peculiar motion as if to dab at her dress. It was there, where the sleeve ballooned from the shoulder, that the blood had spattered. And Abraham had fallen forward so loosely. Dear God! He's been shot!

Another explosion! No. No, it was a knocking. Someone was knocking at the door. She rose drowsily, feeling dizzy, and put a hand on the chair to steady herself. Then both hands went to her hair. She must look a fright!

"One moment!" She said it with the voice of a stranger and moved slowly toward the door. It would be the bundle boy, of course, with the curtains. Where to put them? In one of the trunks, she supposed. She really shouldn't have purchased them.

Not really. But Beatrice was such a sweet child.

She flipped the latch and opened the door. The bundle boy, obscured by the packages he carried and staggering under the load, entered. Mary Lincoln fixed startled bluish-gray eyes on the men behind the boy. Sam Turner, the Grand Pacific manager. And Leonard T. Swett, the prominent attorney who had been one of Abraham's good friends.

The two men stepped across the threshold and Swett bowed slightly. The boy was fiddling with the packages. He managed to set them down quickly and departed. Mary Lincoln's hands flew again to her mussed hair. Then one hand dropped to the mourning brooch.

Swett, tall, spare, muscular and florid-faced, stroked his beard and watched her soberly. She saw, too, the strangeness in Turner's eyes.

"Gentlemen, you must excuse my appearance." She was thinking of the mud on her skirt.

Swett moved to the chair, fidgeting with his hat, and then motioned to it. "Never mind your hair, Mrs. Lincoln. Sit down here. I have some bad news for you."

Daggers of anxiety drove themselves through her. Robert? Something must have happened to Robert. Ah, her poor, fragile boys! The old fear rose in her. Not her last living son? She had believed him to be ill when she left Jacksonville. That was why she had come. She had sensed it. No. No. She had read it somewhere. Robert had been ill.

Mary Lincoln's knees suddenly felt weak. She sat down abruptly, turning startled eyes to Swett. She was vaguely aware that Sam Turner had left the room.

Swett cleared his throat. "Mrs. Lincoln," he said sonorously, "your friends have with great unanimity come to the conclusion that the troubles you have been called to pass through have been too much and have produced mental disease."

The words slapped cruelly at her comprehension. What was this man saying? What did he mean?

"You mean," she said softly, "to say I am crazy, then, do you?"

"Yes." Swett sighed almost as if with relief at having got it into the open. "Yes. I regret to say that is what your friends all think."

Her friends indeed! Mary felt switches of fear and anger now. No friends of hers! These were her enemies—enemies of the Lincoln name! But not Leonard Swett. Could he have changed? Could he be turning against Abraham?

Mary experienced swirls of confusion. What was going on here? She turned to her God. I shall fear no evil, she thought, for thou art with me. She shouted down her shrieking nerves and spoke calmly. "I am much obliged to you, but I am abundantly able to care for myself, and I don't need any aid from such friends. Where is my son Robert? I want him to come here."

"You will see him in court," Swett said bluntly.

In court indeed? Could it be that they had gone this far?

"The court? What . . . court . . . do . . . you . . . mean?" Mary Lincoln's round, smooth face set firmly. "Who says I am insane?"

"Judge Davis says so, and your cousin, John T. Stuart; Robert says so; and I do not want to throw the responsibility of this on others. I say so."

Swett was avoiding her eyes, but his voice was firm with determination. His face swam before her. Swett? Judge Davis? She had long known that they did not care for her. But Abraham—they revered her husband. Something was terribly amiss. Swett's face swam before her. Robert? Robert? Waiting in court . . . ?

Could this be political treachery? Did they want her out of the way?

No, she decided tiredly. It didn't fit. This was . . . she managed a grim little smile. It was almost bipartisan. Robert was a Stalwart Republican, a Grant adherent. Swett and Davis hated Grant and all he stood for.

My last son, she thought tiredly. My last son has left me completely now. Now I truly am all alone. And from deep within her a great sob of anguish and of yearning welled up and up, building as it came, and at last it burst from her. Mary Lincoln felt as if she surely must choke from the ring of cold, menacing hostility now being drawn so closely about her.

Her hand, fluttering nervously, fell to the chatelaine watch, and she thought of Beatrice. It comforted her.

"I have a friend," she said defensively. "I have a friend. That I know."

Chapter 3

WHY HAD HER son forsaken her, his mother? Mary Todd Lincoln rose majestically from her chair in the room which suddenly seemed to be stifling her. There was determination in her stance. It was in her mouth and eyes, too.

She would not yield, she thought. Robert had joined the Pharisees about her. He was a Grant Stalwart, a spoils system man. But why had Swett assumed the role of the Trojan Horse? It drove puzzlement through her again, and she stepped back in confusion. Then she decided. The enemies of Abraham must be at her throat. She must not yield to them.

Avoiding her eyes, Swett pulled from a pocket several letters and offered them to Mary.

"What are these?" she demanded. "I shall not be served by you with any papers. Go away."

"These are letters, Mrs. Lincoln. They have been prepared by five prominent Chicago physicians."

"What have these to do with me?" Mary wanted to know. "I need no physicians now. I need friends to help me."

"They are opinions establishing your insanity, madame," Swett replied coldly. She could see impatience in his eyes.

"My insanity indeed." Mary let rage into her eyes, but her voice remained soft. "I haven't seen these physicians. They do not come to see me. They know nothing about me. What does this mean?"

Swett's mouth set grimly. "It means that you are under arrest, Mrs. Lincoln. Permit me to explain to you that when a person is believed to be insane, an affidavit must be filed in the county court, whereupon a writ is issued. Ordinarily, the sheriff takes this writ and proceeds to arrest the party and take him or her to court. In this case, Robert has made the affidavit. Two officers have come along with me, but I was constrained not to permit your person to be seized by officers and forcibly taken to court. Therefore, I have come in lieu of the officers to request that you go along with me."

Mary Todd Lincoln flatly refused. Was she an animal to be dragged off so abruptly to some Roman holiday? She commenced pacing back and forth before the startled Swett. Could he not see, she demanded, that he and Robert were mere instruments being manipulated by enemies of the very name of Lincoln? No. Absolutely not. She would not submit to this indignity and humiliation. She wanted counsel. She wanted time. She would fight this and she would win.

Swett listened silently, his eyes on the floor. When she had finished, he raised determined eyes to her troubled countenance.

"Nothing in your case remains, madame, but to go with me. You have no alternative. If you insist, then I shall turn you over to the officers and let them take you. There are two carriages waiting downstairs. One of them is mine. The other belongs to the officers. If you choose not to come quietly, I must either seize you forcibly or turn you over to those officers. Rest assured that they will handcuff you if that becomes necessary. Certainly, they will take you to court."

Swett paused and his face grew thoughtful. His voice was softer, almost syrupy, when he spoke. "How much better for you to put on your bonnet and go along with me as you ordinarily would."

"Are there others besides Mr. Turner and the officers?" Mary wanted to know. "Is there a gallery of our enemies drawn up outside to cheer as the widow of Abraham Lincoln is taken forth in chains to the arena?"

She had let the bitterness welling up within her into her soft voice. It was edged with irony now.

"Only Ben Ayer," Swett said. "He waits outside with the officers."

"Ah, Mr. Ayer. Another prominent Chicago lawyer. Does it require such a magnificent array of legal brain power, Mr. Swett, to crucify one little old lady such as Mary Lincoln?"

She watched the blush rise in his face and saw the shade of sadness cross it. He turned his eyes away. His voice seemed muffled. "Mr. Ayer is your son Robert's counsel, Mrs. Lincoln."

"Ah yes, my son Robert. I should say, Mr. Swett, that he needs counsel from above, and not from a mere man whose purposes do seem to fit a pattern of connivances which has not been strange to me since that Good Friday in 1865 when Abraham was shot down. Why have you turned?"

"I am sorry, Mrs. Lincoln, that you are insane, but I must do my duty."

"And you are attending to insane people, are you, Mr. Swett? Allow me to suggest that you go home and take care of your wife, then. I have heard some stories on that subject about her."

Mary turned slowly to study the picture of Abraham on the table. The eyes, she thought, were very sad. His eyes were always sad.

"And you, my husband's friend, would take me and lock me up in an asylum, would you?"

She felt the scalding tears come then. She had hoped to avoid this, but it was too much. Too futile. She raised her hands imploringly, and turned her face upward, so that the tears coursed under her smooth chin now and bathed her throat.

"O God, please return to me my Abraham that I may be delivered from mine enemies. Send him, Good Lord, that he may release me, and drive them away!"

"Please, Mrs. Lincoln, I implore you . . ."

She turned on him abruptly, her eyes flashing.

"Why are you doing this to me, Mr. Swett? What manner of evil is this in you? Why do you, of all people, believe a poor widow to be insane? Why?"

Swett sighed and shifted his weight impatiently. "Well, Mrs. Lincoln, did you not telegraph Dr. Isham several months ago that Robert was sick when, in fact, your son's health was never better? Was that not what you advised him from Jacksonville, Florida? And did you not, that same day, send a telegram to Robert, too, and say to him in it that he should rouse himself and live for his mother? Didn't you? And did not you tell him that you pray every night that he might be spared?"

"Ah, Mr. Swett, and that I do. I do pray every night that my only remaining son be spared. Cannot you understand this great anxiety within me? Yes, even Robert, I fancy, is taken from me now. He is my only son left to me. The others, you see, are dead. They are gone."

"Really, now, Mrs. Lincoln." Swett's voice was filled with impatience. "What does that have to do with the present circumstances?"

"Have you ever had even one son die in your arms, Mr. Swett?"

"No, but . . ."

"I have, sir," Mary said softly. "Eddie was only four then. It was the first of February, a cold and bitter day in 1850. I can remember it so clearly. He was taken ill, you know, in December. They said it was diphtheria. I think only God really knows what it was that came to take him from me. He grew weaker and weaker, and then he died. Of such is the kingdom of Heaven, Mr. Swett. We had that put on his marker, you know. He was so young. So very young to die."

"I am sorry, Mrs. Lincoln. But this is 1875, madame. That was so long ago. Twenty-five years ago, madame."

"It is as yesterday to a mother," Mary said tiredly. The fight was oozing from her now, leaving her limp and exhausted. "Time cannot heal such bruises on a mother's heart, you see. It is a special kind of hell, sir, to watch a child die, a child whose trusting eyes do say to you that he is certain you will not let anything happen to him, you see. A special kind of hell, Mr. Swett. It is the reproach that comes into those eyes with death's calling. No. It is as yesterday, you see. It was yesterday."

Mary paused, going to the window to look out. She was aware of Swett's startled face as he moved quickly toward her. She turned about. He stopped, anxiety across his florid, bearded countenance.

"But I have lost three sons, Mr. Swett. Not one, you understand. Three. Willie was next. He was just twelve, and we were in the White House then. It, too, came in February. It was the twentieth and we were at war in that year. 1862. That horrible war . . ."

"Thirteen years, Mrs. Lincoln."

"Yesterday," she insisted. "It was only yesterday, Mr. Swett. Bilious fever, they called it. He lived only eleven days after being stricken. I remember. Fort Donelson had fallen then to General Grant. Fort Henry, too. It fell first, I think. And then Donelson. Yes. And then Willie. All I have left of him is a withered bouquet. It was in his hand, and I had them fetch it to me. . . ."

"You must not trouble yourself so, madame. We must go. They wait for us at the courtroom."

She ignored him, staring into the kind of distance which reaches back across the years of pain and sorrow.

"Why cannot Robert understand this anxiety for him which possesses me? Lives there a mother gifted with a mother's great love who does not fret within her mind constantly about her children—how they are, how they progress? What is their health? you think. Are they all right? And then to lose three of them! Is this to render immunity, then, to anxiety for the fourth and last one? Is it? There is no vaccination against mother love, Mr. Swett. It is—" she fingered the worn gold wedding ring—"it is eternal, you see, as the love from which it came."

"Your strange horror of fire, madame. Is this not a symptom of lunacy? Why do you say to people that this city will surely burn again?"

"Ah, Mr. Swett. Have I satisfied you, then, concerning my fears for Robert, who now turns on his mother? Is it, then, that only two deaths will buy off such insanity as this? Tad was the sweetest one, you see. I think it was because he was most often hurt. Speech was difficult for him. His cleft palate was his cross in life, and he bore it well, sir. Children jeered at him and mocked him here in Chicago. They

shouted 'Tongue-tied Tad' at him and laughed to see
the pain this brought on his proud little face. God
forgive me if, perhaps, I loved him more. He would
have taken it, but I could not. We moved many times
until, I thought, this land which boasts of freedom,
and this widow of a man who gave that proud boast
shining glory, must seek freedom from mockery on
foreign shores. Is it not ironic, Mr. Swett? The son
of a man they called the Great Emancipator must go
abroad to find freedom from intolerance."

"If you will excuse me, Mrs. Lincoln? That is not
the question here. You see . . ."

"His condition did improve in Europe, Mr. Swett,"
she cut him off. "I saw it first in Germany, at Frankfort on the Main. And in England he had a wonder-
ful tutor. But I became ill. Conditions abroad, you
see, are not so advanced as here, in our country. I
became ill and wanted again to come home. We came
through heavy seas and it was very cold, and Tad
took a cold one day while strolling on the deck. He
died right here in the Clifton House. It was so very
hot. It was in July, you know. So very hot, and yet
Tad was so cold. He just suffocated, my tender, loving Tad. Just could not breathe. His face turned
blue. He was dead."

"But the fire. You have a lunacy about fire. . . ."

"No lunacy," she retorted. "The fire came in

October of that year. It was an omen, perhaps. The fire which burned Chicago down came after my son Tad died here."

"We must get to the courtroom, Mrs. Lincoln. The trial . . ."

"Yes. The trial. My trial has been so long, Mr. Swett. It began on Good Friday in 1865. I remember how packed the theater was, and how the Union soldiers stood about it with their long muskets as if these would keep out the malevolence which seethed about my Abraham. The blood is here. See it here?" She fingered her right sleeve. "Blood of my husband. There was not even a final word. I knew, even as they carried him away. Perhaps if Robert had been there . . . But he was not. He would not come with us. Abraham wanted him to do so, but he would not. He was not there beside me then, and he is not here beside me now."

"We were deeply sorry, Mrs. Lincoln. All of us were sorry. But that is not the question before us now. I must insist, madame, that we leave for the courtroom."

"He died in the line of duty," she said. "He died as those soldiers who went before him. He was a soldier, too. He was the commander in chief. And so I asked for a pension and they put a bill in Congress for it. And this is when the hate was transferred to me. I am sure you remember what happened in our Congress, Mr. Swett. I am the only woman whose name was ever dragged through such mud and mire in those dignified houses which some have called the temples of our democracy. Temples indeed! Vilification! Slander! And in the United States Senate! Oh, I have saved this calumny, Mr. Swett, for I want to remember it. I have the *Congressional Globes* in which those speeches appeared."

Mary moved to the closet and picked up the thumb-worn copies, studying them.

"Hear this villainy, Mr. Swett. Hear this calumny and tell this grieving widow who now has lost four sons if her eccentricities are not well rooted in infamous slanders in our noble Senate. Senator Yates is speaking here, you see. He said: 'There are recollections and memories, sad, silent and deep that I will not recall publicly, which induce me to vote against the bill. A woman should be true to her husband. I will not go into details. I believe that, could Mr. Lincoln speak from the abode of Heaven, he would say as I do. This is not a case where we should extend charity. I happen to know that she and her family all through the war were sympathizers with the rebellion.' This is what our noble Senator Yates told the world about Mary Lincoln, sir. That she was untrue to her eternal love. And that she was a traitorous first lady in the White House!"

"Come now, Mrs. Lincoln. Some men are cruel with words, but you must not carry on so."

"And with deeds as well as words, sir. You come to me and say come with me, Mary Todd Lincoln, and I will take you to a courtroom and then will put you away in a dungeon. You say I am insane because an anger burns at me for those injustices fostered by mine enemies who now sit aside and jeer at what you do. Do you know, sir, that Senator Tipton pointed out that even a dog which had belonged to Abraham would be kept immune to this day from indignity? Why not, then, his poor widow? Am I less than a dog to be treated thus?"

"I must insist, Mrs. Lincoln. I really must."

"Yes, you must, Mr. Swett. I daresay this is for reasons best known to yourself. Yes, I suppose that one may conclude that I am mentally depressed. But insane, Mr. Swett? No. Never!"

"Well, mentally depressed then, Mrs. Lincoln. We must go. We must be going."

"Yes, mentally depressed. Who would not be? Poor Abraham's body was hardly in the grave before that devil's advocate Herndon, his own law partner, mind you, produced the most vicious lies of them all."

"We must overlook Herndon, Mrs. Lincoln. A man addicted as he is to alcohol cannot be mentally sound."

"Yes, overlook such insanity as sears a widow's very soul with its malice, but put that widow into chains for her reactions to it. This is wild and fearful reasoning, Mr. Swett."

Mary returned to the closet and put the thumb-worn *Globes* away.

"I even helped this Herndon," Mary said. "I thought to be kind to him and so I met him in the Nicholas Hotel at Springfield and he pretended to me to be my husband's friend. I turned to him for advice, and I told him, therefore, many family secrets, trusting him with them. I thought his book would be a monument to the memory and the goodness of my dear Abraham, and for this faith he repaid me with malicious treachery. Lies! All lies!"

"Not all, Mrs. Lincoln. It was not such a bad book as that."

Mary was fingering her wedding ring again. "He said Abraham loved Nancy Rutledge better than his own life. This was a vicious fiction. He said that Abraham loved another and had told me so. Do you realize, Mr. Swett, how feminine dignity reels before such mendacious ferocity? He raised a question as to the death of our children and its devilish imputation was aimed at me. He said that Abraham once fled and left me spurned at the altar. He even raised a question as to the legitimacy of Abraham's birth and described him as 'rising from a stagnant, putrid pool.' He called my husband infidel and atheist, my husband whom I have seen on his knees imploring God to give him wisdom for his people."

"Your husband is not on trial here, Mrs. Lincoln. Please control yourself. Come with me as you normally would."

"Ah, but Abraham *is* on trial, Mr. Swett. You and others have put him there, you see, for I am in his shadow constantly."

"I cannot agree with that contention, madame."

"For two thousand pieces of silver," Mary said thoughtfully, "this Lamon bought Herndon's material and under his name he published all of this calumny. His name, you see, but with a pen dipped in villainy by Chauncey Black, the son of a judge who was a well-known enemy of Abraham."

"But friends bought up copies, Mrs. Lincoln, and destroyed them."

"Yes. I know that. But there are others still about. Words such as these once written cannot be recalled, Mr. Swett. These words have woven false threads into the fabric of history. If only one reader believes them, is not Abraham's memory damaged for it?"

"Newspapers called you mad, Mrs. Lincoln, when you wanted to auction off your clothing." Swett was pacing impatiently now.

"Yes. Those were furious articles, Mr. Swett."

"You caused much embarrassment to Robert with those eccentricities."

"Eccentricities indeed! If this was madness, it was merchant madness! Merchants suggested the auction so that I might pay off debts. And why not? People wanted these garments because they loved me, you see. But Robert left me. He scolded me and left me. He was furious at the articles in the newspapers; like a maniac and almost threatened his life. And only dear Tad, who yet lived then, prevented me from taking mine."

Mary sat again, looking at her dress, and she could feel the weight of the folded bonds sewn into the special pocket of her first petticoat. "I have fifty-six thousand dollars' worth of bonds," she said tiredly. "That is what you all are after, I suppose. I know what you want with them."

Swett stopped his pacing and gave her an impatient stare. "I insist."

"Very well." She said it as a deep sigh. Her eyes studied her muddied skirt. "See my dress, Mr. Swett? It is all muddy from shopping. I must change my dress and certainly you would not humiliate me and compel me to undress myself in your presence?"

Swett blushed. "I regret that you should throw the necessity on me, madame. There is no need for a change in your dress. However, whatever comes, it might as well be understood here and now that I am not going to leave you and you must go with me."

"And why won't you leave me alone a moment?" Mary wanted to know.

"Because if I do, Mrs. Lincoln, I am afraid you will jump out of the window."

"It is you, Mr. Swett, who should jump out of the window." Mary rose slowly, studying the large closet in which she had placed the *Congressional Globes*. She moved to it, deciding it would have to do, and entered, closing the door behind her. In the darkness she found the dress she sought and managed to make the change. Then she re-entered the room.

Swett was waiting. A mixture of impatience and anxiety was stamped on his face.

"Will you take my arm, Mrs. Lincoln?" he said. She was putting on her bonnet.

"No, thank you." Mary felt the switches of anger again. "I can walk yet."

They had to wait for the elevator. Mary wondered if Swett would speak further about it out here, in the open, with people about. She decided to change the subject and was still discussing the panic when they reached the steep grade leading to the street. Swett offered to help her into the carriage, but she shrugged him off.

"No," she said abruptly. "I ride with you from compulsion, Mr. Swett, but I beg you not to touch me."

They were silent during the ride to the courtroom. Swett spoke only to answer her question as to where it was. He said it was at North Dearborn Street and West Hubbard. Mary turned, once, to look back. The carriage with two policemen, Sam Turner and Ben Ayer in it followed them at a distance.

They moved quietly through the courthouse to the courtroom. Swett opened the heavy door abruptly and the murmur of voices reached Mary. There were strange men standing about, and she drew back fearfully. Perhaps one of them wanted to kill her, as that crazed one had shot poor Abraham.

"Come right along, Mrs. Lincoln," Swett's syrupy voice urged her. "Robert is in here and I will sit by you."

Fear weakened Mary Lincoln's knees. She felt the perspiration start in her palms. His words did not reassure her, but there was no turning back now. She entered slowly and seated herself in the chair designated by Swett.

She watched as Swett walked across the murmur-filled courtroom toward a man. The man turned, and she saw with a start that it was Robert. Her only living son looked across the courtroom at her and then moved toward her.

"Mother," he said, and she thought his voice quivered just a bit.

"Sit down, my son," she said kindly. "Sit by me in my hour of need."

Chapter 4

MARY TODD LINCOLN sat quietly beside her son in the courtroom commencing to fill with murmuring people and hoped desperately that this was all some terrible dream. She had known such dreams since Abraham had gone, but never one quite so strange as this one. Her small hand went to the mourning brooch with the sad-faced image on it.

Swett moved over to her, and his voice brushed through her whirling thoughts.

"You are entitled to counsel, Mrs. Lincoln," he was saying. "Your old friend, Mr. Arnold, is here. He was your husband's friend, and I imagine that you would rather have him and Robert sit beside you than any stranger?"

Mary Lincoln thought that over. Robert was a stranger now. And Isaac N. Arnold? Was he truly yet a friend? Leonard Swett had been Abraham's friend, too, and now he had turned against her for some strange reason beyond her. Leonard Swett, the man who had placed Abraham's name in nomination right here in Chicago. And now he was soiling that name through her. Was Arnold with them? Should she trust the diminutive lawyer? She decided she would and saw relief in Swett's eyes when she said so.

Mary let her eyes roam about the courtroom. It was filling slowly with curious faces. She reflected grimly that the word must be spreading rapidly throughout the building. The jury box was already filled, she noticed, and as she studied the faces turned toward her, she started in surprise. Most of them she knew, some of them quite well.

She prodded her memory and told herself the names: Lyman Gage, the bank president; J. McGregor Adams of Crerar and Adams Company, the railway supply firm; Mr. Parkhurst and James A. Mason, the prominent foundryman; Charles B. Farwell of the wholesale drygoods firm; Charles Henderson and Mr. Cameron; Thomas Cogswell, the jeweler; William Stewart of Stewart and Aldrich Company; Silas Moore, real estate and loans; Henry Durand of the groceries firm, and a final man whose face Mary could not place. They were Robert's friends, she told herself, not hers.

The soft voice of Isaac N. Arnold penetrated her

thoughts. She managed a faint smile and extended
her hand. He took it gently, bowing slightly, and
kissed it.

"Good day to you, Mrs. Lincoln. It is such a pleasure to see you again, but I am sorry that we must
meet in such circumstances."

Mary was thinking that Isaac Arnold had not
changed. He was the same diminutive, bearded, po-
lite little man with the old school manner. She studied
his eyes and decided he was, indeed, friendly.

"This is the day," she replied soberly, "that my
enemies have been waiting for."

"I suspect, Mrs. Lincoln, that perhaps this is the
day your enemies have been planning for." Arnold's
gentle face was grim; his sharp, even features stiff.

The abrupt pounding of the gavel by the bailiff interrupted them. Mary looked about as persons in the
courtroom rose to their feet. She rose, too, listening
to the bailiff intone: "State of Illinois, County of
Cook, in the County Court of Cook County. This
court will now be in order."

Shock and apprehension raced through her as she
saw the large man in a jurist's robe who entered the
courtroom by the door behind the bailiff and mounted
the bench. Martin R. M. Wallace! It couldn't be!
Was this Democrat who had hated her husband to be
her judge?

Judge Wallace seated himself ponderously and murmurs swept the courtroom as people sat down. Judge Wallace leaned forward toward the bailiff, and Mary could see his lips moving. The bailiff turned, lifting a paper.

"The case of Robert Todd Lincoln versus Mary Todd Lincoln," he droned. A faint sigh seemed to run through the audience. "Application to try the question of insanity of Mary Todd Lincoln."

This time the sigh rose in volume, and Judge Wallace used the gavel vigorously.

"This court will be in order. Expressions from the audience will be dealt with severely." The judge's eyes were on Mary Lincoln now. "The court wishes to observe that the jury has already been impaneled and sworn and that the court is, and has been, ready for this proceeding to begin. Are all of the parties now present and prepared to proceed?"

Arnold flashed a glance at Ayer, who was saying the plaintiff was ready, your honor. He squeezed Mary's small hand and rose slowly; drawing back his coat, thrusting his thumbs into the sleeve openings of his vest, he moved slowly toward the bench.

"If the court please, may counsel for the defense offer the observation that the defendant Mary Lincoln was arrested at one o'clock this day and that it is now but two fifty-five. It is obvious per se that no person could possibly come here in such short order to face such grave charges and be expected to be ready to defend herself against them. For this obvious reason, I move that this trial be recessed until June 19 next in order that my client be given a just and proper period of time in which to prepare her defense."

"The motion is overruled," Judge Wallace droned sonorously. "The hearing will proceed."

"If the court please, your honor." Mary heard the surprise in Arnold's smooth voice. "I move that this hearing be recessed, then, until at least tomorrow at this time in order that we may be given twenty-four hours to prepare for this proceeding."

"The motion is overruled," Judge Wallace intoned. "The hearing will proceed."

Mary watched the flush rise in Arnold's neck and ears. "Your Honor," he was saying, "I am begging this court in the presence of Almighty God for mercy. With that in mind, I move that the court grant a one-hour recess in order that counsel for the defense may familiarize himself with the serious charges brought here."

"Mr. Arnold," Judge Wallace said, "there is not going to be a recess. Not even for five minutes. This court has waited long enough. This bench has appointed you, Mr. Arnold, to defend this defendant. Since you have long been a friend of the family, this court must take notice that you should be familiar with the actions of this defendant and with the charges brought here as a result of those actions."

"I am familiar, your honor," Arnold said, "with the fact that this honorable woman and erstwhile first lady is being pilfered of statutory rights. If the court please, we are dealing with a most delicate subject in a most indelicate manner. I move for a fifteen-minute recess."

"Motion denied. Proceed with the hearing."

"A question, if the court pleases." Arnold's smooth voice was edged with the anger of frustration now.

"Proceed, Mr. Arnold."

"How is it that this jury was impaneled without counsel for the defense being given opportunity to challenge a single member? How is it that this jury is sworn? May I observe, again, that this poor little lady was arrested less than two hours ago in her room and brought here under threat of force? What sort of jury is this? Is this jury impaneled to weigh and decide, or has it been impaneled to convict?"

Mary listened to the murmur of excitement ripple through the growing audience. The gavel demanded silence. "Mr. Arnold, the court admonishes you to watch your tongue." Mary thought the judge sounded perturbed.

"May I have a copy of the charges preferred against my client?"

"If there is no objection?" Judge Wallace stared at Ayer. Mary watched her son's lawyer shake his head. "Your request is granted."

Arnold wanted to know if the defense was to enjoy the privilege of producing friendly witnesses and might cross-examine hostile witnesses. Judge Wallace said these privileges would be granted.

"And if the court please, I ask again, your honor, if it is not most unusual for a jury to be impaneled without giving the defense the right to question prospective jurors, or the statutory privilege of exercising challenge?"

Ayer rose quickly. "Your honor, we find nothing wrong with interrogation of jurymen by Mr. Arnold in so far as their qualifications are concerned."

Arnold managed an exaggerated bow toward Ayer and moved toward the jury box. Mary watched the jurymen shuffle nervously.

Arnold had halted before Juror Cogswell. "Will you state your full name and business for the court, Mr. Cogswell?"

"Thomas Cogswell, associated with the firm of Cogswell-Weber Company, jewelers."

"Yes. And do you know Mary Todd Lincoln?"

"Only through the trade."

"Through the trade? And what do you know of her through the trade, Mr. Cogswell?"

"She is a little slow in paying her bills, sir."

"Ah, yes. And I suppose that during this present panic, Mr. Cogswell, all your other customers are most prompt in paying their obligations?"

"No, sir. We have many persons on our books."

"Thank you, Mr. Cogswell. Now, Dr. Blake . . ." Arnold had halted before the man whose face was strange to Mary. "You are the city physician of Chicago. Is that correct?"

"Yes."

"And you frequently treat people who are in mental distress?"

"Oh, no, sir."

"Infrequently, then?"

"Hardly ever, sir."

"Hardly ever? That means you treat such persons intermittently, I assume?"

"Well, as a matter of fact, only once . . ."

"Ah, yes. Only once. Now, Doctor, in view of such broad experience, do you profess to be qualified to judge if a person is sane or not?"

"No, sir. I am a trained medical administrator."

Mary turned curious eyes to the audience. She

saw some men writing and realized that these must
be newspapermen. Arnold's voice droned on as he
moved through the jury.

Mary closed her eyes. Weariness assailed her. I
wonder, she thought, how long it will take? How
long will it take them to do this to me?

She turned sober eyes back to Arnold as he completed his questioning. He had moved back before
the bench.

"If the court pleases, the defense finds this entire
jury objectionable and requests that new jurors be
called and that defendant's counsel be permitted to
examine each one."

"Mr. Arnold," Judge Wallace grated, "your repu-
tation is known to this court, but we are not going
to deal here today with inferences or innuendoes.
This jury has been fairly impaneled and is ready to
hear this case, and it will hear this case."

"In the name of common decency, your honor, I
ask that the court take notice of the violations of this
defendant's statutory rights which have taken place
here. I suggest, sir, that it begs of remedy."

"The court cannot see," Judge Wallace said,
"where the statutory rights of this defendant have
been denied. We will now hear from Mr. Ayer, counsel for the petitioner."

Mary watched Arnold's shoulders droop visibly. He turned, strode to her and dropped into his chair. His eyes were flashing.

Ben Ayer had risen slowly to his feet. Now he turned toward the jury and raised his voice.

"If the court please, we have here today the case of an anguished and embarrassed son who has been forced to represent that his mother, Mary Todd Lincoln, is insane and that for her benefit and the safety of the community she should be confined in an asylum. This woman has in her possession a large sum of money, and it is known beyond all doubt that she had been profligate with money in the past. This woman is absolutely *non compos mentis*—incapable of managing her substantial estate. The truth of these allegations will be proved beyond all doubt. It will be shown that Mary Todd Lincoln's mind has failed beneath the weight of the blows which have fallen on her, and then she must be declared insane and a conservator appointed to manage her estate. Testimony will disclose that the defendant is emotionally unstable and as a result suffers from hallucinations which induce abnormal conduct."

Ayer finished and returned to his chair.

Arnold rose slowly. "The defense offers no statement at this time, your honor, but requests that this jury again be sworn, in the presence of the accused, and that each juror weigh carefully the wording of the oath which is given to them."

Color rose in Judge Wallace's face. "The jury has been once sworn and this is sufficient. Mr. Ayer will proceed without further delay."

Ayer rose. "The petitioner now calls Dr. Willis Danforth."

Mary watched the bailiff open a door and then return with a tall, bearded man following him. Mary recognized the physician. He seemed to avoid her eyes as he was being sworn, and then he sat down in the witness chair.

Ayer moved quickly to a position beside the first witness so that he faced the jury.

"State your name please."

"Willis Danforth."

"And your occupation, sir?"

"I am a doctor, a professor of surgery and a gynecologist at Chicago Homeopathic College."

"You are acquainted with Mrs. Lincoln, Doctor?"

"Yes. Professionally. I treated her for several weeks in November of 1873 for fever and nervous derangement of the head."

"Objection!" Arnold had leaped to his feet. "I object to the use of the word derangement."

"Objection overruled. Proceed, Mr. Ayer." Judge Wallace looked bored.

"Did you observe anything of particular interest at that time, Doctor?"

Doctor Danforth said indeed he did. He had observed at the time indications of mental disturbance. "She had strange imaginings."

"Such as what, Doctor?"

"Well, she thought that someone was at work at her head and that an Indian was removing bones from her face." Murmuring swept through the courtroom and Danforth halted. Judge Wallace pounded for silence.

Danforth continued: "And pulling wires from her eyes. I visited her again in September 1874, and found a debility of her nervous system. She complained to me that someone was taking steel springs from her head and would not let her rest and that she was going to die soon. Within a few days, she said. She said her husband had told her that. She also imagined that she heard raps upon a table and that these conveyed to her the time of her death. She sat at the table and asked questions and repeated answers which she claimed the table was giving her."

"Would you say, Doctor, that this derangement was the result of any condition of her body?"

"No, sir, I would not. She was not diseased."

"And have you seen her, Doctor, since last year?"

"Yes. I called on her at the Grand Pacific a week

ago and she appeared to be in excellent health. She spoke of her stay in Jacksonville, Florida, and of the pleasant time she had there. Her former hallucinations seemed to have passed. She said, however, that she was not well and that an attempt was made to poison her as she came north at a wayside station near Jacksonville. She said she discovered poison in her coffee."

"Did you see any traces of poison about her, sir?"

"I did not."

"And what was your opinion then, sir?"

"That Mary Lincoln was and is insane."

Mary listened to a sigh of gasps about the courtroom. She stared at Danforth, but he avoided her eyes.

"Cross-examine," Judge Wallace said.

Arnold took the place where Ayer had stood. "I will ask you, Doctor, if it is not true that when a woman reaches a certain age chemical changes occur within her body which are accompanied by melancholia?"

"That is true."

"And is Mrs. Lincoln at, or beyond that age?"

"I would say so. Yes."

"Now, Doctor, you have testified that in 1873 you treated Mrs. Lincoln for a 'nervous derangement of the head'?"

"Yes."

"Not of the mind, or of the brain? But of the head?"

"That is what I said."

"Such as a stiff neck, Doctor?"

"I object!" Ayer leaped to his feet.

"Objection sustained. What the witness said speaks for itself."

Arnold managed a significant glance at the jury. "Now, Doctor, is it not true that Mrs. Lincoln told you that she *felt* as if someone were pulling bones from her face, such as an Indian scalping her, and that she *felt* ill, and that she *felt* as if someone might have poisoned her?"

"I do not remember her exact words."

"I see. Then you are not certain beyond doubt just what it was that she said. Is that right?"

"Objection. The witness is having words put in his mouth."

"Objection sustained."

Arnold threw another grim look at the jury. "I will ask you, Doctor, whether you have ever reported any of these findings to the plaintiff, Robert Todd Lincoln?"

"Objection."

"Objection sustained. Mr. Lincoln is not on trial here."

"Mr. Robert Lincoln is not, if the court please," Arnold shot back. "Mr. Abraham Lincoln seems to be." He paused. "That will be all, Doctor. Thank you."

"The plaintiff calls Samuel M. Turner."

Arnold sat down slowly as if he was tired. Mary felt his hand squeeze hers reassuringly. She managed a grim smile.

Ayer waited until Turner had been sworn.

"State your name and occupation, please."

"Samuel M. Turner, manager of the Grand Pacific Hotel."

"You are acquainted with the defendant, Mary Todd Lincoln?"

"Yes, since last March fifteenth, when she came to my hotel."

"And have you noticed anything unusual about her actions since that time?"

"Yes, sir. She visited me at the office on the first of April. She had a shawl wrapped about her head and she said for me to come into the reception room with her as she had something to say to me. She said something was wrong about the house—that she could hear strange noises in the rooms. I went with her and heard nothing, and when I was about to leave she turned to me, scared-like, and said not to leave her; she was afraid to be left alone."

"And what did you do then, Mr. Turner?"

"Why, I left her in charge of a female employee and returned to my office."

"And was that the end of it?"

"Oh, no, sir. I had hardly reached my office when a messenger came and told me that Mrs. Lincoln was at the elevator and wished to see me. She told me this time that there was a strange man in the corridor and that he was going to molest her. I went up to her rooms with her and walked through them, but I found no strange men. Mrs. Lincoln was much excited, though, and said that she would like to go to some lady boarder's room so that she might be safe. I escorted her to Mrs. Dodge's room, but Mrs. Dodge was at dinner. I left her and told her I would return soon."

"Yes. And was that the end of it?"

"No, sir. She called me again and I went to her and found her quite exercised and wild in appearance. She repeated to me her fears."

"And what did you then conclude, Mr. Turner?"

"Objection! This calls for a conclusion by the witness." Arnold's voice cracked like a whip.

"Overruled. This witness is permitted to draw a conclusion from such activities."

"I figured she was deranged, sir."

"Your witness, Mr. Arnold."

Arnold moved again to the place vacated by Ayer.

"Now, Mr. Turner, you say that when you explored the living area of Mrs. Lincoln you found no strange man. Is that right?"

"That is correct."

"Did you see anyone at all, as a matter of fact?"

"Yes, sir, I believe so. That is, I must have seen some persons."

"And are Pinkerton men strangers to you, Mr. Turner?"

"I don't know what you mean, sir."

"I mean are Pinkerton men—the ones who have been watching Mrs. Lincoln and following her—are they strangers to you."

"No, sir."

"But they might be strange to Mrs. Lincoln. Is that right?"

"Objection!" Ayer leaped to his feet. "Mr. Turner cannot testify concerning how something may appear to Mrs. Lincoln."

"Objection sustained," Judge Wallace droned.

"Very well." Arnold tugged at one ear. "You do know, Mr. Turner, that Pinkerton men were watching Mrs. Lincoln?"

"Yes, sir. I knew that."

"And they were given the run of your establishment?"

"I beg your pardon?"

"I said, they were free to roam your hotel at will."

"I suppose so."

"And they watched Mrs. Lincoln's every move?"

"That is what they were hired to do."

"And in view of the constant peeping by these men at Mrs. Lincoln, do you still regard it as a symptom of derangement in her that she was frightened?"

"Well, I can understand it better, since you put it that way."

"Thank you, Mr. Turner. That is all."

Mrs. Allen was the next witness. Mary watched with sober eyes as she took the stand. Mrs. Allen was very abrupt with her. Mary did not like Mrs. Allen. Ayer dispensed quickly with the introduction of the witness; her name and the fact that she was the housekeeper at the hotel.

"Do you consider Mrs. Lincoln to be normal, Mrs. Allen?" Ayer's voice was softly encouraging.

"No, sir, I sure don't."

"And why not, Mrs. Allen?"

"The lady is so awful nervous, and she's feared of a small window in her room. Says it means bad for her. Last Wednesday, the madame mixed several kinds of medicine and swallowed it and she has a large closet filled with packages. She sure ought to be put away, sir, and cared for right like."

"Your witness, Mr. Arnold."

Smiling faintly, Ayer returned to his seat beside
Robert Lincoln.

"Now, Mrs. Allen," Arnold began softly, "you say
that Mrs. Lincoln mixed several kinds of medicine
together and then swallowed the mixture?"

"Yes, sir."

"And do you know, Mrs. Allen, what Mrs. Lincoln's instructions were regarding that medicine?"

"No, sir."

"You do not know whether or not the mixing of
this medicine was, in fact, prescribed by the attending physician?"

"No, sir."

"Then, in fact, Mrs. Allen, Mrs. Lincoln may
simply have been following a doctor's orders."

"Yes, sir. I guess so."

"You guess so, you say? You guessed then, too,
didn't you, Mrs. Allen? Do you say, now, that this
mixing of medicine indicated insanity?"

"I guess not, sir."

"Now, Mrs. Allen, you testified, I believe, that
Mrs. Lincoln has a large closet filled with packages?"

"Yes, sir."

"Where do you keep packages, Mrs. Allen?"

"Why, I . . ."

"As a matter of fact, any neat housekeeper, and I

am sure you are quite neat, would keep packages in
a closet rather than leave them lying about a room.
Isn't that right?"

"Yes, sir. I guess it is."

"You are quite a guesser, Mrs. Allen. That is all."

Maggie Gavin, the next witness, moved slowly to
the stand, her plain, dull face showing fear. Mary
Lincoln felt sorry for her. She meant well, Mary
thought, but was so fearful of losing her job at the
hotel that she bowed to everyone's slightest whim.

Ayer was stern and firm with her. "Now, Miss
Gavin, have you ever seen Mrs. Lincoln act
strangely?"

"Yes, sir."

"Will you tell the court about it?"

"Well, sir, she said once she heard people speaking
to her through the wall, she did. She was very wor-
ried about her son, and once she told me to listen to
voices she heard through the floor. She said a man
had taken her pocketbook, but I found it in a bureau
drawer. Then she called me to the window and
pointed to smoke coming from a chimney on the
building next door and said the city was burning.
She's bought lots of packages and several new trunks
lately."

"Yes. Is there anything else?"

"Well, sir, once she said she was afraid to stay in

her room and she went to Mr. Robert's room in her nightdress."

"And to what conclusion did these activities by Mrs. Lincoln lead you?"

"I ain't sure o' what you said, sir."

"I said, what do you think of Mrs. Lincoln?"

"She's batty, sir. Just plain batty."

"Thank you, Miss Gavin. Your witness, Mr. Arnold."

"My dear Miss Gavin," Arnold began softly, "you are a chambermaid. Is that correct?"

"Yes, sir."

"And you work in the hotel in which Mrs. Lincoln resides?"

"Yes, sir."

"And each room in that hotel is soundproofed?"

"Oh, no, sir." Maggie Gavin's plain face looked surprised.

"Mrs. Lincoln's room is soundproofed then?"

"No, sir."

"Is it possible to hear through the walls?"

"Yes, sir. I suppose so."

"Well, can you or can't you?"

"You can, sir."

"Now, Miss Gavin, since we have established that Mrs. Lincoln might very well have heard voices from the walls, is there . . ."

"Objection!" Ayer looked indignant. "That has not been established. I ask that the witness' answer be stricken from the record."

Judge Wallace sustained the objection and ordered the clerk to strike the answer.

"I will ask you, Miss Gavin," Arnold said slowly as if controlling anger, "if you have ever heard voices through the walls at the hotel?"

"Yes, sir."

"And have you heard noises on the floor below through the floor?"

"Yes, sir."

"And have you ever looked up suddenly and seen smoke and concluded that something was burning?"

"Yes, sir."

"Do you consider that this makes you insane, Miss Gavin?"

"Oh, no, sir! No, indeed!"

"Thank you, Miss Gavin. That will be all."

Mary recognized John, the waiter at the Grand Pacific, as the next witness. His name, he told Ayer, was John Fitzhenry, and he was second waiter at the Grand Pacific. She remembered, as he told of it, how she had asked him to summon Mr. Turner that day when she had seen strange men watching her and was afraid.

Arnold said he had no cross-examination. "This

man has testified," he said grimly, "that Mrs. Lincoln became fearful of strange men and called for the hotel manager. He has not testified that such an action indicates insanity."

Judge Wallace rapped his gavel sharply. "The clerk will strike Mr. Arnold's remarks. I warn you again, Counselor, that this court will not tolerate these flippant asides of yours. Watch your tongue."

Charles Dodge, cashier of the hotel, simply corroborated the waiter's statements, Mary thought. He did not say he regarded her as crazy. She sighed, watching as Arnold moved to cross-examine and wondered why he bothered. The man had said nothing. Absolutely nothing.

"Mr. Dodge," Arnold began slowly, "you recited your testimony very well."

"Thank you, sir."

"Who drilled you in it?" Arnold's voice lashed like a whip now.

"Objection!" Ayer leaped to his feet. "That is, if the court please, a leading question."

"Objection sustained."

"Now, Mr. Dodge, as cashier of the Grand Pacific you would know the owner of it. Is that correct?"

Mary's eyes widened. What was Isaac Arnold up to?

"Yes, sir," Dodge said. "I know the owner, sir."

"By name?"

"Yes, sir."

"And by sight?"

"Yes, sir."

"You know him well?"

"Yes, sir. Not socially, sir. But I speak with him often."

"Yes. Now, Mr. Dodge, will you tell the court the name of the owner of the Grand Pacific Hotel?"

"Mr. Lyman Gage, sir."

"Yes. And do you see Mr. Gage in this room?"

"Yes, sir."

"Please tell the court where you see Mr. Gage."

"He is on the jury."

"Very well, Mr. Dodge. Now. Did Mr. Gage ask you to come here today?"

"He was the first to speak to me about it."

"I see. Others have spoken to you about it?"

"Yes, sir."

"And you discussed with them what you would say?"

"Yes, sir."

"Objection!" Ayer's voice came late. He rose angrily. "Mr. Arnold seeks to intimidate a witness."

"Objection sustained. Mr. Arnold, you will confine your questioning to facts relating to the matter at hand."

"If the court please, your honor," Arnold snapped, "the defense regards any conspiracy with witnesses as related directly to the matter at hand."

Murmuring rose in the room again. Judge Wallace used his gavel furiously. "Another such outburst, Mr. Arnold, and I shall consider a contempt of court citation to be required."

"Very well, your honor. Now, Mr. Dodge, as an employee of Mr. Gage, you are inclined to be responsive to his wishes. Is that correct?"

"Yes, sir, I suppose so."

"And these other employees who have appeared as witnesses against Mrs. Lincoln also would feel similarly, I imagine?"

"I would imagine so, sir."

"Thank you, Mr. Dodge. No further questions."

Mary was surprised to see Mr. Seaton, the United States Express Company agent. She remembered, however, that she had, indeed, sent eleven trunks to Milwaukee last April. It had been her plan, she remembered, to spend an extended vacation in Milwaukee. Was that, too, to be held as insanity?

Arnold disposed of Seaton briefly.

"Mr. Seaton, you have sent many trunks for many people, I take it?"

"Yes, sir."

"Including those of famous ladies of the theater?"

"Yes, sir."

"And those famous ladies usually had only one or two trunks?"

"No, sir. Some of them had as many as a dozen or more."

"They were staying here for some time, then?"

"For a week maybe. Maybe two weeks."

"And you considered them quite sane?"

"Yes, sir."

"Even though they carried possibly a score of trunks with them for only a one or two weeks' stay?"

"Yes, sir. They were first ladies of the stage, sir. They had to dress the part, sir."

"And this is the first lady of our country, Mr. Seaton. Do you not think she should dress the part, too?"

"I suppose so, sir."

"Do you think her insane because she shipped eleven trunks to a place where she intended to spend the entire summer?"

"No, sir. Her manner was strange, sir."

"But not insane?"

"Strange, sir. I did not say the lady was insane."

"Thank you, Mr. Seaton. I do not think her insane either. No more questions."

Dr. Isham was the next witness. Mary guessed that he would testify concerning the telegram she had sent

him from Jacksonville. She guessed correctly. The
doctor said he had received the telegram March 12
last and that it said: "My belief is my son is sick. I
start for Chicago tomorrow." He said Robert was not
ill at the time and that he telegraphed her to that
effect. He said Robert, too, telegraphed her to remain in Florida.

"Mr. Lincoln also received a telegraph. It read:
'My dearly beloved son, Robert T. Lincoln: Rouse
yourself and live for your mother. You are all I have;
from this hour, all I have is yours. I pray every night
that you may be spared to your mother.' "

Arnold's cross-examination again was brief.

"Doctor, how did you come by the telegram sent
to Robert Lincoln?"

"He gave it to me."

"I see." Arnold turned to look directly at Robert
Lincoln. "You are, Doctor, the nephew of Mr. Lincoln's law partner, is that right?"

"Yes. That is correct."

"And you have discussed this trial with your uncle
and Mr. Lincoln?"

"Objection!" Ayer's face looked troubled. "I repeat, your honor, that Mr. Lincoln is not on trial
here."

"Mr. Lincoln is on trial before a higher court than
this one, Mr. Ayer."

"I ask the court to compel my colleague," Ayer said bluntly, "to confine his remarks to the case at hand."

"And the court so orders, Mr. Ayer." Judge Wallace was glowering at Arnold.

"I have no more questions, your honor, if I cannot explore the intricacies of relationship and motive which have precipitated this piece of infamy."

Arnold sat down disgustedly.

Ayer rose and walked to the witness chair. He stood to one side and placed his hand upon the back of it. Then he said slowly, "I now call Robert Todd Lincoln as a witness."

Mary felt stabs of pain as her only living son rose and walked to the witness chair. What would he say about her? Why was he doing this to her? Why?

She shifted in her chair, her thoughts whirling. The space beside her was empty now. Her son had left her to side against her. Mary Todd Lincoln looked at her son and felt the wash of tears down her cheeks.

Chapter 5

ROBERT TODD LINCOLN sat down slowly in the witness chair, as if he was very tired. His eyes were large, and Mary thought she saw fear and pain in them. His face was pale and drawn. He gripped the arms of the witness chair nervously.

Robert averted his eyes from her, but she could see that they were moist.

"Your name, sir?"

"Robert Todd Lincoln."

"And your relationship to this case?"

"I am the petitioner."

Ayer turned to look at Mary. "And this defendant is related to you?"

"She is." Robert's voice was muffled. "She is my mother."

"Do you have a statement which you wish to make to the court at this time?"

"I do."

"Please proceed, Mr. Lincoln."

Robert spoke slowly, and his voice seemed muffled. Only the slowness of his speech reminded her of Abraham, Mary thought. Otherwise, he was completely different. It was as if he were a stranger. Indeed, she thought, he was a stranger. She had never understood Robert at all.

Robert was reviewing the death of his three brothers—her sons—and that anguished period after his father was shot down. It was most unpleasant, he was saying, for a son to have to face up to it, but the strain had been too much for his dear mother. Her mind had cracked. She was quite insane.

Arnold's soft voice interrupted her concentration on Robert's words. She turned to look into his small, bearded face. The eyes were gravely thoughtful.

"Robert is a Stalwart, isn't he, Mary?"

"Why . . ." Mary studied the small man intently. What did this have to do with her sanity? "Yes, he is an ardent supporter of General Grant."

"Do you approve?" Arnold's face was intent as he waited for her answer.

"I have never approved of General Grant," Mary said abruptly, "and I certainly do not approve of his

spoils system and of those things which are being
done with aid from the White House."

"Have you ever heard Robert's name mentioned in
connection with political matters?"

"There has been some talk," Mary said thoughtfully. "He is so young, though. And he professes to
be disinterested."

"Yes," Arnold said. "So did Abraham." He
studied her intently. "Did you know that Swett and
Judge Davis are anti-Stalwarts? Liberal Republicans?"

"I had heard that," Mary said. "I can understand
it. They were very devoted to Abraham and under-
standably proud of his integrity."

"Yes," Arnold said thoughtfully. "They would resent any use of the Lincoln name to further the
spoilers' policies, wouldn't they?"

And with that cryptic observation, Arnold said no
more. They turned to listen to Robert's testimony
again.

Robert was now telling about his mother's concern
for him when she insisted that he was ill. He did not
understand why she had said that. He hadn't been
ill in years. Realization that his mother was insane
had been most sad to contemplate. That was why he
had taken this action. It would be to her best interests to be put away for treatment. As it was now she

was a menace to herself. There was no mercenary angle to this. He did not want her money. He had money in trust for her, as a matter of fact.

"When she came up from Florida, I met her at the railroad car and was quite startled to find her looking fit and in good health. She did not even seem fatigued by the trip. I asked her if she would not like to come to my house and stay, but she said no, and went to the hotel. I accompanied her, and we had supper together. She told me that someone had attempted to poison her at the first breakfast she took after departing from Jacksonville. She said it was put into her coffee. I took a room adjoining hers that night and she slept well. But on subsequent nights, she became restless and repeatedly came to my door in her nightdress and aroused me by rapping. Twice in one night she did this, and asked to sleep in my room. I gave her my bed and slept on the lounge."

Robert sighed and twisted nervously in the chair. Then he bowed his head into one hand.

"I summoned Dr. Isham to attend to her. That was about the time she ceased tapping at my door. I had told her rather sternly that if she persisted, I would leave the hotel. I went to her room April first and found her but slightly dressed, and she left the room and the next I knew of her she was going down to the office in an elevator. I had the elevator stopped and sought to persuade her to return to her room. She said I was being impertinent by interfering and would not leave the elevator. I put my arms about her, thinking to force her to leave, and she commenced screaming. She said, 'You are going to murder me.' After a while, she said a man she had met in Florida had taken her pocketbook and that he was going to return it at five o'clock. Then she sat down by the wall and said he was talking to her and began carrying on a conversation.

"I called on her during the last week in April, and she told me that all of Chicago was going to be burned and that she was going to send her trunks to some country town. She kept her trunks in the Fidelity Safe Deposit Company's building, you see. She said she had changed her mind about sending them to Milwaukee. She said it was too near Oshkosh, and there had been a terrible fire there the night before. She told me that my house would be the only one saved. I suggested to her, then, that she leave her trunks with me."

Robert hesitated, as if thinking.

"And did anything occur the following Sunday, Mr. Lincoln?"

"Yes. Yes, the following Sunday she showed to me securities valued at fifty-seven thousand dollars which she carried in her pocket. She had been spending large sums of money; she bought six hundred dollars' worth of lace curtains, three watches costing four hundred fifty dollars, other jewelry worth seven hundred dollars, soaps and perfumeries worth two hundred dollars, and a whole piece of silk."

"Yes. Now tell the court, Mr. Lincoln, whether, in your opinion, Mrs. Mary Lincoln is sane?"

"She is without doubt insane," Robert said. His voice was muffled. Mary felt shock clear through her to hear him say it this way.

"Now, Mr. Lincoln," Ayer said, "when you came to that sad conclusion, what course did you take?"

"I had a conference with my mother's cousin, Mayor Stuart of Springfield, and Judge Davis of the Supreme Court. All advised me to take this course."

"Do you regard it as safe," Ayer wanted to know, "to allow her to remain longer unrestrained?"

"I do not," Robert said. "She has long been a source of great anxiety to me. I have had Pinkerton men watching her for the past three weeks. Their only duty has been to look after her when she went on the street. After all, she had no real home, and declined to visit my house because of a misunderstanding between her and my wife. My mother has always been kind to me, but I fear she has been of unsound mind since my father was shot. She has been irresponsible for at least ten years. She is eccentric and unmanageable. There was no reason on earth for her recent purchases. Her trunks are filled with dresses which she has never worn, and, as you know, she has not worn jewelry since my father's death."

"That is all, Mr. Lincoln. Your witness, Mr. Arnold."

Arnold rose slowly, turned deliberately and patted Mary's hand. She had dried her tears and was staring at Robert with a stunned expression in her eyes. He would not look at her, and this hurt her as much, she thought, as what he had just said.

Arnold took his position and studied Robert soberly for possibly a full minute. The courtroom suddenly was very quiet. Mary wished someone would make some noise. It seemed unbearably quiet.

"Mr. Lincoln," Arnold said softly, at last, "I wish you to look at your mother."

Mary watched as Robert's eyes lifted slowly to her bluish-gray ones. She felt the tears start again.

"You do love your mother very much, don't you, Mr. Lincoln?"

"Yes." His voice sounded husky.

"Are you aware, Mr. Lincoln, that your mother read in a Florida newspaper that you were ill?"

"No. I had not heard that."

"Didn't you ask your mother how she had come by such misinformation?"

"No, sir."

"Why not?"

"I don't know. It just didn't occur to me."

"You said, in your lengthy statement, Mr. Lincoln, that you did not want any money from your mother. Is that correct?"

"Yes."

"You are certain of that?"

"Yes. Positive."

"Now I ask you, Mr. Lincoln, if it is not a fact that in December 1868, in a letter to your mother, who then was living at Frankfort on the Main in Germany, you requested the loan of approximately fifty-one thousand dollars' worth of 1881 bonds, which loan was to be used in connection with the construction here, in Chicago, of twenty-eight houses for speculative building purposes?"

"That was different, sir. It offered ten per cent on the money for five years."

"I ask you, Mr. Lincoln, if that is true?"

"It is."

"Yes. How, then, do you reconcile that with your statement that you did not want any money from your mother?"

"I meant recently."

"How recently, sir?"

"Since she has been insane."

"Did you not testify, Mr. Lincoln, that your mother has, in your opinion, been of unsound mind for the past ten years?"

"I think that is what I said."

"Do you want the clerk to read what you said?"

"No. That is what I said."

"Then, Mr. Lincoln, that would mean that you sought to obtain a large sum of money from your mother believing her to be insane?"

"Object! Object! Object!" Ayer stormed toward the bench. "I respectfully suggest once again to the court that Mr. Lincoln is not on trial here."

"And I suggest, Mr. Ayer, that Mr. Lincoln is on trial. He has made the allegation that his mother is insane, involving a question of both her good name and her freedom. This is a sanity trial, I grant you, but I am not certain in my own mind just who is of unsound mind here. The Good Lord knows that certainly it is not Mary Todd Lincoln!" Arnold's face was white with anger and his voice snapped and popped at Ayer. Ayer withdrew several steps.

"The court," Judge Wallace said sonorously, "will sustain the objection by counsel for the plaintiff." Wallace glowered at Arnold but said no more.

"You said, Mr. Lincoln, that you have money in trust for your mother?"

"Yes."

"Objection." Ayer was on his feet again. "If your honor please, I see no valid reason for Mr. Arnold's pursuit of this line of questioning."

Judge Wallace stared uncertainly at Arnold.

"Your honor," Arnold said, in a voice of outraged innocence, "I am only following a line of questioning suggested by the witness himself. I did not bring up the subject of this money. Mr. Lincoln volunteered it. If it was germane to the case then, your honor, why is it not germane now?"

"Objection overruled," Judge Wallace decided reluctantly.

"Is it not a fact, Mr. Lincoln, that this money which you claim to have in trust for your mother is, in fact, an obligation to her which you are paying at one hundred twenty-five dollars per month?"

"My mother calls it a loan, I suppose."

"She gave to you a certain large sum of money, Mr. Lincoln, and you are returning it at the rate of one hundred twenty-five dollars monthly. Is that right?"

"Yes."

"Then I cannot see where Mrs. Lincoln errs in terming it a loan. Now, Mr. Lincoln, is it not true that you raged at your mother and then left her in a fit of anger when she sought to sell some of her clothing to collectors in order to raise money to pay certain debts?"

"I became quite exercised, yes."

"Why, Mr. Lincoln?"

"I was a young attorney establishing a practice. It would have caused me professional embarrassment. Besides, she did not need the clothing in the first place."

"No more than you needed twenty-eight houses, Mr. Lincoln?"

Ayer bellowed an objection. Judge Wallace said, "Sustained."

"So you objected to your mother selling her clothing on the grounds of personal embarrassment?"

"Yes. It would have hurt my career."

"Your career, Mr. Lincoln?"

"Yes."

"And who would you say launched you on that career, Mr. Lincoln?"

"Why, I suppose it was my mother."

"Yes. Your mother. She prepared you for and used her influence to get you into Harvard, did she not?"

"Yes."

"She insisted that you finish your education there before taking up arms in the great war?"

"Yes." Robert's voice seemed more muffled now. "And then she demanded for you a commission and a place as an officer on the staff of General Grant?"

"Yes."

"She has never raised one hand against furtherance of your career, but, in fact, has consistently advanced that career. Is that right?"

"Yes. I suppose so."

"We are not dealing in suppositions, Mr. Lincoln. Has she or hasn't she?"

"She has."

"Yes. Now, Mr. Lincoln. Why did you not reciprocate?"

"I do not follow you, sir."

"Why did you not discuss your mother's eccentricities with her instead of hatching this plot four days ago and declining to notify her of it until one o'clock today?"

"Objection!" Ayer's face was beet-red. In contrast Robert Lincoln looked very pale.

"Objection sustained."

"She gave you time to finish your education, Mr. Lincoln," Arnold persisted. "Why did you not give her time to prepare a defense?"

"Objection," Ayer roared again. "Mr. Arnold is badgering the witness."

"Objection sustained," Judge Wallace said. "Mr. Arnold, you will cease this line of questioning."

"Very well, your honor." Arnold tucked a clenched fist into the beard beneath his chin and studied the witness thoughtfully.

"Mr. Lincoln," he said softly, "you have said that there was a misunderstanding between your wife and your mother."

"Yes."

"Of what nature?"

"I cannot say."

"And have you sought to resolve that misunderstanding?"

"No, sir."

"Why not?"

"I cannot say. I have been very busy."

"So busy, Mr. Lincoln, that you cannot seek to straighten out a misunderstanding which prevents your mother from coming into her only remaining son's home?"

"I do not understand it," he said. "They used to have such affection for one another."

"Have you tried to understand it, Mr. Lincoln?"

"I suppose not."

"I see. You would not say, then, that the antagonism of Mary Harlan, your wife, to Mary Todd Lincoln, your mother, is due to the influence of your wife's father, the senator?"

The flush rose slowly in Robert Lincoln's face.

"I would prefer not to say."

"I see. Very well, Mr. Lincoln. Now, you believe, do you, that your mother suffered hallucinations when she told you that someone sought to poison her?"

"Yes."

"Do you find it so strange that there is hostility to even the name of Lincoln south of the Mason-Dixon line?"

"No. But I do not believe that anyone tried to poison her."

"But you do not know, do you, Mr. Lincoln?"

"Not of a certainty."

"Yes. Not of a certainty. And you would not take her word for it?"

"I could not."

"I see. And why not?"

"I question her reliability, her mental competence."

"Oh. You question her reliability. Now, Mr. Lincoln, you said that your mother showed to you fifty-seven thousand dollars' worth of securities?"

"Yes. In bonds."

"You are certain of the amount, Mr. Lincoln?"

"I believe so."

"Why?"

"My mother gave me the figure."

"Ah. Your mother told you?"

"Yes."

"And you believed her?"

"I had no reason to doubt her."

"Ah. You do not doubt her ability to count, but you doubt her reliability about the attempt to poison her?"

"Well, I . . ."

"Objection!" Ayer was glaring at Arnold.

"I will overrule that objection, Mr. Ayer. Proceed, Mr. Arnold."

"Thank you, your honor." Arnold turned back to Robert. "You complained, Mr. Lincoln, of your mother's purchases of perfumeries, jewelry and other items?"

"I mentioned them."

"Because you thought it indicated insanity?"

"Yes."

"Did it ever occur to you, Mr. Lincoln, that perhaps your mother purchased those items to give them to certain friends?"

"No."

"Were you not aware, during these years, that your mother was very lonely and wanted love and friendship?"

"I have been quite busy."

"Yes, Mr. Lincoln, you have." Arnold studied him. "But you were not too busy to handle Tad's money when a court had decreed that Judge Davis should handle his estate, were you?"

Robert looked startled. He darted a glance at Mary. Her smooth countenance was expressionless.

"Judge Davis was quite busy."

"We have any number of very busy people involved here, don't we, Mr. Lincoln?"

Robert did not answer, but a flush rose in his face.

"Now, Mr. Lincoln, when your mother waived her right under law to two thirds of Tad's estate, did you not advise Judge Davis that 'This is very generous on her part'?"

"I did. It was generous."

"Ah. Then it was generosity?"

"I looked at it that way."

"You did not regard it as insanity when she gave something to you, then? Only when she gave something to others?"

"Objection! Mr. Arnold is not propounding questions. He is drawing conclusions."

"Sustained," Judge Wallace said.

"Very well. I need not draw conclusions. I apologize to the court," Arnold said. His voice was tinged with irony. "The conclusion here speaks for itself."

After a pause he went on. "Mr. Lincoln, am I correct in recalling that you said you have had Pinkerton
men watching your mother?"

"Yes."

"Night and day?"

"Practically, yes."

"And yet you find it strange that she has seen
them and assumed that someone was seeking to do
her harm?"

"I did not say that."

"You say that these men were to protect your
mother?"

"Yes. They were to look after her."

"You did not employ them, then, to gather evidence
for this trial?"

"Of course not!"

"But much of the testimony elicited here today
comes from the reports of those men. Is that right?"

"I suppose so."

"And who has been paying for the Pinkerton service, Mr. Lincoln?"

"There has been no payment yet."

"I see. And now if your mother is put away, Mr.
Lincoln, will you pay this obligation from her
money?"

"Objection!" Ayer was watching the bench.

"Sustained," Judge Wallace decided. "The witness cannot testify to something which has not yet been done."

"If your honor please," Arnold said, "the witness can testify to his intent to do something."

"Mr. Arnold, this witness does not yet have control of his mother's money and there has been no indication that he will have."

"Very well, your honor." Arnold turned back to Robert Lincoln. "Now, Mr. Lincoln, assuming that your dear mother does have some eccentricities, don't you believe that the villainous lies of Herndon and Lamon concerning your late father contributed to them?"

"I imagine that they did."

"And she has stood alone against these enemies?"

"Objection! Mr. Arnold propounds a question based on an assumption."

"Objection sustained."

Arnold paused and threw a long, significant glance at the jury. Then he threw back his shoulders.

"The defense has no further use of Mr. Lincoln, your honor." Arnold turned abruptly and sat down beside Mary. There was a grim little smile on his lips.

Mary Lincoln clutched at his sleeve.

"I am glad you are finished with him, Isaac. Let us not torture the poor boy any more."

"But this is your defense, Mrs. Lincoln!" Arnold studied her and she saw the surprise in his eyes.

"He will suffer a lifetime for having done this now," Mary said. "He is more sensitive than perceptive, I fear. Let us give him as much peace of mind as possible."

"Would you trade your freedom for this, then, my dear lady?"

"Yes. It is done," Mary said. "My day will come. The day will come when Leonard Swett himself will set me free."

The next witness gave his name as J. R. Albertson and said he was a salesman for Matson and Company. Mary recognized him as the man who had looked at her so strangely when she purchased the chatelaine watch this morning. Under questioning by Ayer, he said he knew Mrs. Lincoln, that she had come to the store and made expensive and reckless purchases, and acted in a queer way generally.

Again Arnold dealt with the witness briefly.

"You say, Mr. Albertson, that Mrs. Lincoln acted in a queer way generally?"

"Yes, sir."

"Will you describe what you mean?"

"Well, she was in a hurry, like this morning, and she paid for the watch she bought."

"I see. You find it strange for people to pay for merchandise these days, do you?"

"No, sir. I mean, she always seemed troubled, almost sneaky."

"I see. As if someone might be following her and watching her every move?"

"Yes."

"And in view of Mr. Lincoln's testimony that Pinkerton men were watching her night and day, can you now understand her actions?"

"Yes, sir, I believe I can."

"Thank you. That will be all."

The next witness was J. B. Stone, a salesman with Allen and Mackey, and he testified that he sold Mrs. Lincoln three hundred dollars' worth of lace curtains. "I thought she did not know what she was doing at this time, though."

Arnold studied the man gravely.

"But you sold her the curtains anyway?"

"Yes."

"Why?"

"Business is business, sir."

"Yes. Business is business, Mr. Stone. I have no further questions for such lack of integrity as this."

Mary watched Dr. Davis take the stand. He had

been kind to her. Why would he testify against her?
Ayer was looking grim.

"Now, Dr. Davis, you have examined Mrs. Lincoln, have you not?"

"Yes."

"And what was your conclusion?"

"She had no symptoms of epilepsy, but I did not regard her as safe to be left alone."

"You visited her, I believe, years ago, Doctor?"

"Yes."

"And what did you find then?"

"She was eccentric, sir, as many of us are. She was extremely nervous. But . . ." Dr. Davis hesitated, and his eyes sought out Mary Lincoln. "I saw nothing in her to indicate unsoundness of mind."

Ayer looked stunned. "No further questions."

Judge Wallace looked at Arnold. Arnold rose. "If the court please, the defense has no further questions of a witness for the plaintiff who speaks against the plaintiff's case."

The next four witnesses were brief. W. H. Wooster, the Wabash Avenue jeweler, said Mrs. Lincoln purchased watches and spectacles from him, contracting a bill of three hundred dollars, but that the goods were taken to Robert and he returned them. J. S. Townsend of a jewelry firm and E. T. Moulton of a drygoods house disclosed similar dealings. T. C. Mattock detailed dealings with Mrs. Lincoln and said he thought her insane.

Arnold waived cross-examination, but looked interested, Mary thought, when Dr. Johnson took the stand to testify that he was satisfied, from evidence he had heard, that she was deranged.

Arnold's voice was disarmingly soft.

"You say, Doctor, that you believe my client to be insane from the evidence you have heard?"

"Yes."

"And do you know the rule of hearsay evidence, Doctor?"

"No, sir."

"It is not admissible," Arnold snapped. "I move that this man's statements be stricken for that reason."

"Motion denied." Judge Wallace managed a bored look. "A doctor is entitled to form conclusions from what he has heard."

"But is he entitled to make a diagnosis on the basis of hearsay, your honor?" Arnold asked grimly.

Then he returned to his chair and listened to Dr. Smith, the next witness. The doctor said he had listened to the evidence and observed Mrs. Lincoln's actions, and was of the opinion that her mind was not sound. Ayer was satisfied with that.

Arnold moved slowly to Dr. Smith, studying him thoughtfully.

"You are Dr. Charles Gilman Smith?"

"That is my name, yes."

"You have treated Mrs. Lincoln professionally?"

"I have not, sir."

"I see. Then you, too, are basing your diagnosis on what you have been told?"

"Yes. What I have been told and what I have heard here."

"And you have assumed that all of this testimony is true?"

"Yes." The doctor looked surprised. Ayer's objection thundered through the room. The judge said, "Sustained."

"You doctored Tad Lincoln, did you not?"

"Yes."

"And other youngsters?"

"Yes."

"And you always diagnose their illnesses from what you are told?"

"Of course not. I examine them."

"Ah, so? And why is that?"

"Why, I want to be sure before prescribing medicine."

"But you do not care to exercise such caution now

when the remedy to be prescribed is confinement behind barred doors, is that it?"

"Objection," Ayer bellowed.

"Sustained," Judge Wallace said.

"During that time when you were doctoring Tad Lincoln, how did Mrs. Lincoln's actions strike you, Doctor?" Arnold was ignoring Ayer.

"She was quite nervous and upset."

"Would you say she was a typically distraught mother?"

"Yes."

"No more than that?"

"No."

"Now, Dr. Smith, to what do you attribute these eccentricities and this nervousness which some seek to indict as insanity?"

"Objection!" Ayer turned angrily to Arnold. "Counsel for the defense is again putting words in a witness' mouth."

"It seems only fair," Arnold growled. "A sort of reciprocal privilege." He managed a surprised look. "I am astounded that Mr. Ayer should object to that practice, but I shall rephrase the question."

"Proceed, Mr. Arnold," Judge Wallace said.

"I will ask you, Dr. Smith, to what do you attribute the present condition of Mrs. Lincoln?"

"If she is not of sound mind, sir, I attribute it to recent events in her history."

"Thank you, Doctor. That is all."

Ayer rose slowly. "If the court please, I shall now recall Mr. Robert Lincoln."

"Is this necessary, sir?" Judge Wallace looked startled.

"There is a final question which we desire, for the benefit of the Lincoln name, to have answered," Ayer said.

"Very well, Mr. Ayer. Proceed."

Robert moved slowly to the witness chair. His eyes were downcast.

"Now, Mr. Lincoln," Ayer said, "will you tell the court whether or not insanity is hereditary in your family."

"It is not," Robert said in a low voice.

"And will you tell us your mother's age?"

"She is fifty-six," Robert said.

"That is all, sir," Ayer said. "The plaintiff rests."

"I assume that there are no witnesses for the defense?" Judge Wallace inquired smugly.

Arnold rose to his feet and walked slowly toward the bench, and Mary's eyes followed him.

"That would seem to be a safe assumption, your honor, since my client and I have been denied opportunity to summon friendly witnesses. However, even within the narrow limits of these unduly harsh and penalizing restrictions imposed on us, we have one witness."

Mary felt surprise wash through her. Where had Arnold obtained a witness? Her eyes went to Leonard Swett's face. It was a surprised and troubled countenance.

"The defense now calls Mary Todd Lincoln," Arnold said.

Chapter 6

ARNOLD MOVED to help her as Mary Lincoln stepped up onto the small platform and sat down in the witness chair. She was watching his face and his broad wink startled her. Swett was still staring at her and Robert had raised his head slowly to do so too. Mary turned her eyes straight ahead and waited.

"Now, my dear," Arnold said softly, "I will ask you if it is not true that you are Mary Todd Lincoln, widow of our great president?"

Mary said yes softly and Arnold encouraged her to speak louder.

"Yes," she said.

"And you were sitting beside him when he was shot down and his blood was on your dress."

"Yes. Right here it was." Mary fingered a sleeve,

121

feeling the old splinters of grief being driven through her.

"And before that dreadful day you had lost two children and seven years later you lost a third son."

"Yes."

"Now, Mrs. Lincoln, I will ask you if you did not rather expect that Robert would look after your interests after these tragic occurrences?"

"No," she said, watching surprise cross Swett's face. "No. Not Robert. He tended to remain aloof from me."

"And did he ever consult you on business matters?"

"Only when he wanted money."

"Only when he wanted money," Arnold repeated. "Yes. Now I will ask you, Mrs. Lincoln, if you were given any notice previous to about one o'clock this afternoon that this sanity action was to be taken against you by your son?"

"No. I had no idea."

"But you knew men were following you? Spying on you?"

"I was aware that strange men were constantly following me, yes."

"And it troubled you?"

"Yes. Since Abraham's death, you see, I have had a fear of strange men."

"Yes. I see. Now you have heard your son testify

that these men were following you for your protection?"

"Yes."

"Did he tell you that Pinkerton men had been assigned to maintain surveillance on you?"

"No."

"And when you told him that strange men were following you, did he not then inform you in order to relieve your mind and alleviate your fears?"

"No. He said I was imagining things."

"I see. And you lived in the Grand Pacific Hotel and not your son's home while here?"

"Yes."

"Why, Mrs. Lincoln?"

"Robert's wife, Mary Harlan, does not like me. I would not have felt comfortable."

"You would not have been made to feel at home in your only surviving son's house?"

"I would not have felt at home there. That is correct."

"And so you have been alone, for all intents and purposes, since Tad's death, then."

"Yes."

"Very lonely?"

"Very."

"And you have sought friends."

"I have found friends," she said. "I have my sister,

Elizabeth, at Springfield, and her husband, Ninian Edwards."

"Then why did you not go there, my dear?"

"Memories," Mary said, feeling grief twist her face again. She fingered the gold ring on her finger. "Abraham and I were married there, in that house on the hill. Sometimes it seems as if it were but yesterday."

"I see," Arnold said softly. "But you have, on occasions, stayed with them."

"Yes."

"And did they ever question your sanity?"

"No. Never."

"And do you question your sanity, Mary Lincoln?"

"Of course not. I am quite capable of managing my own affairs."

"Robert's only intimate conversations with you, then, in these years since Abraham's death, has concerned money?"

"Primarily, yes."

"And do you think now that money is the reason for the present proceeding?"

"I would rather not answer that, Mr. Arnold."

"You do not want to tell the world that your son seeks to put you away simply to get your money?"

"Must I answer that question, sir? Must I?"

"No," Arnold said. "I apologize. I do not believe

that the question requires a response from you, madame. Your silence is more eloquent than words."

Arnold turned to Swett and Ayer. "Your witness, Mr. Ayer."

Ben Ayer rose and said he had no questions. The judge eyed Arnold questioningly. Arnold said the defense rested. Mary returned to her seat and watched Leonard Swett rise and move to the jurors to pace slowly back and forth before them.

"Gentlemen of the jury," Swett intoned ponderously, "there falls upon me now the painful task of summarizing for you the testimony in this delicate case; testimony which demonstrates beyond all doubt that Mrs. Lincoln is, indeed, insane. I say to you that in the opinion of her most intimate friends, this poor woman has been insane since the assassination, and that the weight of her woes has been too great for her mind to bear. Recently, as she grew more unsound in her actions, Judge Davis, John T. Stuart and the physicians who had been consulted, and who have testified, advised that the present action was not only proper, but would, in fact, be a kindness to this aggrieved woman. We can understand and sympathize with her condition, gentlemen, for no other woman in our national history has been asked to carry such a cross. And yet, the question before us is not one of whether Mary Todd Lincoln can be excused for her condition. The question goes to that condition itself. Is she or is she not insane? That is the only question which this jury must decide. I therefore call upon this jury to render the only possible verdict indicated by the testimony, and without delay."

Arnold rose slowly as Swett sat down. He moved to the position vacated by the burly lawyer and commenced pacing back and forth before the jurors in thoughtful silence. At last he paused to face them, and he spoke.

"Gentlemen of the jury, what insanity is there, I ask you, in seeking the friendship of others? What madness is there in being kind to people? What unsoundness? If this be madness, gentlemen, then let us have more of it in this world, for this is the madness of Christ. This is what he brought to the world. Love is the most powerful force in all of this world, gentlemen. Without love, the world would be completely mad. And woman, born of man, seeks love. It is a food of the soul, and without it, the feminine heart pines away to dust; withers coldly.

"Mary Todd Lincoln brought four sons into this world, gentlemen, and her mother love was about them as a shield. And one by one, three of them who loved her were taken from her. Between the loss of her second son and her third one, a husband doomed to martyrdom but destined for immortality fell beside her so very close that his life blood spilled upon her garments.

"It is, perhaps, possible for us to visualize the horror of that moment, gentlemen, but I fancy that not one of us can know the anguish for this woman, let alone the persistent terror which followed; fear that another madman, armed and gushing wild Latin phrases, might seek to strike down also the lonely widow of a giant among men who fell for a cause which, thank God, he lived to see free thousands from chains of iron laced with intolerance.

"But she must live on, you see, for there were two sons left to her then. She lived for them. And then Tad was taken from her and she turned to Robert, a woman alone, standing in a shadow of greatness which falls across all of us; standing alone in that shadow in the bitter ashes of what had been her life. And as she turned to this last surviving son to give him and his wife her love and affection, where was the return of it? Where did reciprocal love and affection flee now? Where was this protective arm of a son which should have been about her? Where could the widow of the Great Emancipator go? The kind of intolerance which her prince of freedom for all men hated now seethed about her, and she was required to face it alone.

"Ah, gentlemen, we have heard here today words

which have the sound of a slattern's gossip and we are asked to swallow them as the gospel truth. We have heard phrases which glitter with hard malice and which have the ring of careful calculation. We have heard of voices through walls and through floors, and we have heard testimony that it is madness for Mary Todd Lincoln to hear such things, but quite normal for others to hear them. We have heard an only surviving son brand his mother as quite mad since that dark Good Friday in 1865 when Abraham Lincoln was shot down. And yet, we have heard that same son testify that his mother was sufficiently sane, in his opinion, that he might correspond with her regarding a loan of money for speculative purposes. We have heard him say that a misunderstanding barred his mother from the threshold of his home, and that he was too busy to seek to resolve this misunderstanding.

"Is it so strange, then, that Mary Todd Lincoln sought friendship and compassion and understanding from others? Where else could she turn? Three sons were dead and Abraham was dead, and her only surviving son did not want her about because he feared that her eccentricities might embarrass him and harm the career on which she had launched him.

"I remember my good friend, Abraham Lincoln, as he stood tall and straight at the Capitol, only weeks before he was shot down, and told his country how he hoped to sew up the grave wounds inflicted on his people by civil war. That was in March of 1865 and he was delivering his second inaugural address. It is a curious thing, gentlemen, and most fortunate for us, I believe, that we can know from what he said there how he would react today with regard to this grave matter which now confronts us here. How? How can we know this, you ask?

"Ah, gentlemen! In Abraham Lincoln, as in but few other men since Christ, were rooted the qualities of faith and hope and charity. And his greatest quality was the greatest one, you see. Sweet charity! How would he react indeed? Permit me to recall for you his magnanimous words: 'With malice toward none; with charity for all; with firmness in the right, as God gives us to see the right, let us strive on to finish the work we are in; to bind up the nation's wounds; to care for him who shall have borne the battle, and for his widow, and his orphan . . .' Yes, gentlemen. His widow and his orphan. He spoke eloquently for the widows of others who fell before him. He championed them. I ask you, in the name of Heaven above, can we do less today for the poor little widow of the man who made that plea?"

Not once had Arnold moved from his position before the jury. Now, with an almost imperceptible bow indicating that he was finished, he turned slowly, walked to the seat beside Mary and sat down. She saw beads of sweat on his forehead. Then she turned, at the sound of Judge Wallace's gavel, aware of a murmuring in the courtroom. It ceased.

Judge Wallace fixed stern eyes on the jurors.

"The court desires to instruct this jury that the sole question to be decided by it is the question of whether or not Mrs. Lincoln is, in fact, insane, and should be sent to an asylum. The jury will now retire to deliberate its verdict."

Arnold was quiet as the jury filed out. Mary felt numb. Simply numb. She watched Robert rise and walk to Leonard Swett. They conversed in undertones, both of them glancing occasionally at her. Then Robert came to her and extended his hand, and to her it was more as if she were some acquaintance than his mother. She took his hand limply, thinking that she really had nothing to say to him. Splinters of anger began to race through her. She rose, drawing herself up erectly.

"Robert," she said gravely. "I did not think you would do this."

She watched as Robert bowed his head. His shoulders shook. He wept. Swett approached quickly, moving between Mary and her son.

"You must understand, Mrs. Lincoln," he said

smoothly, "that this is for your own good. No one means you any harm."

"I am not persuaded by you, Mr. Swett," Mary said coldly, "but I shall try to endure these persecutions."

The murmuring in the courtroom ceased as the jury returned, and this sudden silence halted any further conversation with Swett. Mary Lincoln seated herself slowly, studying the faces of the jurors. They were peculiarly set, she thought. She told herself: *It is against me. They will find against me.*

Judge Wallace wielded his gavel vigorously and Mary wondered why. There was no noise in the courtroom, none at all. The shuffling of feet and the nervous coughs had stopped. It was as if everyone was holding his breath.

"Has the jury reached a verdict, Mr. Gage?"

"We have, your honor."

"Read the verdict, Mr. Gage."

Lyman Gage rose slowly, and the paper he held in his hand betrayed his trembling. He cleared his throat nervously.

" 'We, the undersigned, jurors in the case of Mary Lincoln who is alleged to be insane, having heard the evidence adduced, are satisfied that the said Mary Lincoln is insane . . .' "

Sighing rippled through the room. People were stir-
ring now. Mary could see the newspapermen. They
were whispering excitedly among themselves. Judge
Wallace rapped the gavel angrily. The noise subsided.

" '. . . is insane, and is a fit person to be sent to a
State Hospital for the Insane: that she is a resident
of the County of Cook, in the State of Illinois; that her
age is fifty-six years; that her disease is of unknown
duration; that the cause is unknown; that the disease
is not with her hereditary; that she is not subject to
epilepsy: that she does not manifest homicidal or
suicidal tendencies, and that she is not a pauper.' "
Gage read his own and the other eleven signatures.
Then he sat down.

Arnold had turned to Mary before the reading of
the verdict was completed.

"I feel deep shame, Mrs. Lincoln," he said, "that
anyone should do this to you."

"It is all right, Mr. Arnold. Perhaps they will send
me away, but it will not be for long." She eyed Arnold levelly. "I know that you have done your best,
but I doubt that even my Abraham could have
changed this verdict."

Swett had gone to the bench and was conversing
with Judge Wallace. People were streaming from the
courtroom now, and Mary thought that it had become
a hollow, deserted place again. Arnold rose, excused

himself and strode to the Swett-Wallace conference. He returned shortly, announcing that it had been decided to send Mary to Bellevue Place Sanatorium at Batavia, Illinois, owned and operated by Dr. R. J. Patterson.

Swett was conferring again with Robert. Now he turned and moved to Mary.

"Mrs. Lincoln," he said, "you have fifty-six thousand dollars in money and bonds on your person, and one of the unpleasant necessities of this case is that you must surrender them. I could easily obtain a court order, or even have the sheriff take them forcibly from you, but I sincerely hope that you will not make that necessary. Will you not give them properly to Robert?"

Mary looked about for Arnold. He was standing near by, receiving from the clerk a court order for her delivery to an officer. She heard him ask for duplicates.

Mary turned grimly to Swett. "No," she said. "Robert cannot now have anything that belongs to me."

"Here is Mr. Arnold," Swett said, gesturing towad the diminutive counselor. "Won't you surrender them to him?"

"I will not here," Mary said. "They are in my underclothing. Certainly, Mr. Swett, you would not be indelicate to me in the presence of these others. Please take me to my room. It is so hot in here."

"Very well, Mrs. Lincoln." Swett sighed. "I will be glad to take you to your room. Nothing remains but these bonds. Now if you will promise me that after you get there you will give them to Mr. Arnold, we will go there."

Mary said she promised that. "May we go now, please?"

Only once during the ride did she speak up. She turned to Arnold, saying, "Mr. Arnold, I have always been very careful about my money matters. There is no danger that anything will happen to the bonds. I am very much fatigued. I need rest. Suppose you come down tomorrow and we will talk this matter over."

Arnold's face was grim and pale. He flashed a glance at Swett and then looked away, and Mary felt defeated. They did not speak of it again until Swett had closed the door of her room behind them. Then he turned to her.

"Mrs. Lincoln, you promised as a lady at the court that if I would not permit those sheriffs to be rude towards you, you would give the bonds to Mr. Arnold as soon as we came to the room. Now, I am compelled to exact the performance of that promise."

Arnold studied Swett. "There should be a receipt given," he said.

"Yes." Swett nodded agreeably. "I shall go and get some paper."

He left the room and Mary looked at Arnold with tears in her eyes. "What shall I do?"

"Compose yourself, dear lady. There is little which can be done now." Arnold's voice was edged with determination. "But do not fret. We shall win this one yet. It will take time, now, my dear."

Swett returned, sat down and wrote out a receipt.

"Read the receipt," Mary commanded.

Swett complied. " 'Received of Mary Lincoln fifty thousand dollars.' "

"Fifty-six thousand dollars," Mary corrected.

"I beg your pardon." Swett wrote another receipt, read it to her and stood up. "Now, Mrs. Lincoln, the receipt is all right, but we haven't got any bonds."

Mary felt the tears coming again. She rose.

"And you are not satisfied with locking me up in an insane asylum, but now you are going to rob me of all I have on earth? My husband is dead, and my children are dead, and these bonds I have saved for my necessities in my old age; now you are going to rob me of them?"

"Please, Mrs. Lincoln." Swett looked embarrassed

and uncomfortable. "It is for your own good. We do not seek to rob you."

"Yes," she said. "Yes. It is robbery. You are robbing me."

Mary felt defeated. Arnold nodded to her when she looked at him again. She shrugged and moved to the other side of the room. Wearily, as if the hem were some great weight, she lifted her outer skirt and tugged at the pocket sewn into the top petticoat.

"Mr. Arnold," she said at last, "will you help me please?" Her voice was flat and toneless.

Arnold moved to her, knelt, and commenced struggling to extricate the bonds from the pocket. At last, he cast a glance upward at Mary. She nodded. He grasped the pocket firmly and ripped it free.

"It is done," Mary Lincoln said. And in that moment, she would have given anything to see the cheerful, kind, sweet face of her friend, Beatrice.

Chapter 7

"WE ARE AS STRANGERS now," Mary Lincoln said.
"Robert comes to see me regularly each week, but he
comes as a stranger. I think that I no longer know
him."

"We were dumbfounded," the tall, handsome
woman sitting across from Mary said. "Absolutely
dumbfounded. We came, of course, as soon as your
letter arrived. I fear that James and I both thought
at first blush that perhaps . . . perhaps you were . . ."

"Yes," Mary said tiredly, nodding. "I can imagine."

"It was after we read your letter," the woman said,
"that we became convinced that this is an infamous
outrage. Then we examined the transcript and discovered the unusual aspects of the entire affair."

"It was a political trial," Judge James B. Bradwell
growled. "There is a political tinge to it."

Mary experienced faint surprise. These were strong words from another judge.

"I sensed it too," Mary said. She sighed. "I have not followed such things closely since . . . since Abraham left me, but I did, indeed, sense it. But it doesn't make sense, James. No sense at all."

Myra Bradwell said it seemed that way to her, too. "After all, Judge Davis was never really a Republican. He calls himself an independent, and now he is breaking completely with the party in his anger at the Grant people. Leonard Swett, I am sure, is no Stalwart, either. He reveres the memory of your great husband, Mary, and he detests the Grant Stalwarts and all that they stand for."

"Not Robert, though," Mary said. "He thinks the sun rises and sets on Lys Grant. He is really very close to the general." Mary managed to keep her dislike for Grant from her voice. She paused, studying James and Myra Bradwell, and thanked God for friends such as these. They were, after all, a most influential couple, one of the most influential in all of Illinois.

"It doesn't fit, does it?" Mary said. "Why should friends of Abraham Lincoln choose to do this to his widow? There is too much of a mixture of Stalwart and Reformist and Independent here."

"By George!" Judge Bradwell socked one fist into

an open palm and then commenced stroking his beard. "Of course! That's it! Why did it not occur to me before?" He rose and commenced pacing back and forth. "How blind we have been!"

"James! What is it? What are you trying to say?" Myra Bradwell rose from her chair to stare at her husband. Mary watched the tall judge curiously.

"Of course it was political. Of course!" Judge Bradwell's voice was tense with suppressed excitement. He moved to Mary. "My dear lady, isn't it true that politicians around Grant have shown signs of using Robert's name for the political prestige of the Lincoln label on their shoddy doings?"

Mary grimaced. She said yes, that was true. "Robert is becoming increasingly active in the Stalwart ranks. Some say they are grooming him for the Presidency some years hence."

"And who would be most interested in destroying him then?"

Mary experienced slivers of surprise and understanding. "Why, the men who loved Abraham and cherished his goodness and his integrity."

"Yes!" Judge Bradwell said emphatically. "You see?"

Understanding was flashing across the intelligent features of Myra Bradwell, but Mary's whirling thoughts refused to settle down. She stammered something and Judge Bradwell placed a hand softly upon her arm.

"My dear Mrs. Lincoln," he said, "they seek to destroy Robert, your son, through you. When the Stalwart regime is faded and worn with its own shoddiness, they would use a fresh new face and the Lincoln name as their champion. They would use the name of Lincoln to carry their banner and keep them in the White House."

"Yes," Mary agreed slowly, "that is entirely possible. Even most probable."

"And Swett and Davis and such friends of Abraham would resent this cynical exploitation of the Great Emancipator's immortal name," Judge Bradwell said. "They are clever, resourceful and experienced politicians. They have demonstrated heretofore that they will stoop to most anything to win."

"Yes," Mary said, thinking of the convention of 1860. "Yes, I understand that."

"And how far could a man bearing even the Lincoln name go," the judge demanded triumphantly, "if they could say of him that he sent his mother—the lonely widow of his great father—to an asylum?"

Mary Lincoln winced at the word asylum, but her small hands gripped the chair arms until her knuckles were white.

"I see," she said, and her voice was filled with sadness. "I see." And, she told herself, she did see. Old Villain Davis was such a maneuverer. "It was Judge Davis' work," she said. "It fits."

"Davis," Judge Bradwell said, snorting disdainfully. "A judge of the highest court in our land. Swett, lawyer; officer of the court. Stuart, a blood relative. And Robert. Your son, my poor, dear, betrayed woman, succumbed to their blandishments because of your money. They baited a political deathtrap with your bonds."

"It is just the kind of trick Old Villain Davis would think of," Mary said. Anger burned through her slowly. How could they have persuaded Robert to turn against his own mother? She voiced the question aloud.

"My dear lady," Judge Bradwell said. "It was you yourself who suggested the mercenary motive. I simply chose to look a little deeper."

"Robert has always been rather foolish about money," Mary said. "Search for wealth is a compelling force in his life."

"He was named conservator of your estate," Judge Bradwell said with quiet significance.

Mary Lincoln felt twists of anguish now. "My son," she said. "My only son."

Judge Bradwell bowed his head. "I am sorry, dear lady."

Mary heard a sob. It was Myra Bradwell. "How cruel," Myra said. "How terribly cruel!"

"It is a mother's risk," Mary said slowly. "I remember Abraham saying that to me after Willie died." Wistfully she touched the worn gold ring. "How could this come from such love as ours?" She bowed her head.

Myra Bradwell was staring at her husband. "We must go and confront Swett with this," she said. "We must bring this into the open."

"And advance the Stalwart cause? Make martyrs of the spoilers' wing?" Judge Bradwell shook his head. "No, my dear. There is a risk of that."

"What then?" Myra wanted to know. Mary listened intently.

"We must get Mary out of this place first," Judge Bradwell said.

"Placed in someone's care?"

"Yes," the judge said.

"Elizabeth and dear, dear Ninian," Mary said slowly.

"Of course," the judge said.

"Back to Springfield, where we were wed," Mary said, fingering the ring again. Her voice sounded distant.

"But will they agree?" Myra said.

"I think they will," Judge Bradwell said grimly.

"I think Swett will bend every effort when we confront him with his secret."

"And Dr. Patterson?" Mary wanted to know.

"He must stick to his original diagnosis," Judge Bradwell said. "He must. But he can hardly oppose a trial release."

"Yes. And then we must write letters," Myra said. Her lively features were set determinedly. "Scores of letters. We must write to all of our friends in the East. We must heap scorn and condemnation upon this Robert Lincoln."

Judge Bradwell was looking thoughtful. He sat slowly. "Yes," he agreed, "but there is more. The timing is important. We must gear the court action to the next Republican convention. The Reformists are growing quite strong. Swett and the others could not oppose the action to . . ." Judge Bradwell hesitated, smiling at Mary, "to restore you to sanity, my dear."

Myra nodded slowly. "I see. If they have a strong candidate in the running, it would jeopardize his chances."

"The Stalwarts will run Blaine," Judge Bradwell said. "Old Judge Davis might like to do something, as he tried to do in 1872, but he's not big enough." Judge Bradwell grinned. "Politically, I mean."

Myra Bradwell chuckled. "Of course." Mary

smiled, thinking of Judge Davis' tremendous bulk.

"The Stalwarts will try to force a shift to a compromise candidate," Bradwell said. "That must be their strategy. They have no one with which to counter Blaine. They must rely on a dark horse."

"When will they meet?" Mary eyed Judge Bradwell inquisitively.

"Next June," he said. "Patience, dear lady."

"Nearly a year," Mary said slowly, and there was dismay in her voice. She sighed. "I shall wait," she said, "and write letters."

"Your friends will free you, my dear," Myra Bradwell said.

"My friends," Mary said, savoring the word. She stared at the couple grimly. "Leonard Swett himself must set me free."

"Leonard Swett it will be," Judge Bradwell said.

"If he refuses?" Mary wanted to know.

"At the expense of his law practice, his whole career?" Judge Bradwell said grimly. Mary shuddered at the naked fury in the big jurist's voice.

"When we are finished with him," Myra Bradwell said, "he will be begging for the opportunity of freeing you, my dear."

And Mary Lincoln told herself that, now, she could wait.

"We have much to do, my dear," Judge Bradwell

said, as they said their good-bys. "We shall go to work immediately to get you to Springfield. We'll go directly to Ninian and Elizabeth and have them make the necessary request."

"About Judge Wallace . . ." Mary began, but Judge Bradwell cut her off.

"Leave him to me, my dear. I am sure he will appreciate the significance of what I have reserved to say to him."

"And Dr. Patterson?" Mary said.

"Can hardly choose to dispute the judgment of such esteemed gentlemen as Swett, Robert, Davis and the honorable judge," Judge Bradwell growled.

Mary Lincoln told herself a month later, after Beatrice had come and wept and left her the *Tribune,* that Judge Bradwell had, indeed, called the turn of it. Dr. Patterson, apparently irked at publicity growing from Ninian's request and from the Bradwell correspondence, had sought to defend himself in a letter to the newspaper. As Mary studied the letter, she told herself: He has the unmitigated gall to tell the world that I am yet possessed by insanity which did not have me in the first place. But he has made a sorry mistake, for in this letter he has predicted how I will act. Therefore, I shan't act that way at all. I shall prove him wrong.

Mary laid the newspaper down and turned her

mind back to the day they had brought her here. There were physicians in the private car of the railroad president, but she had ignored them to feast her eyes on the lovely scenery of the Fox River Valley, burgeoning with the brilliant greens and pastel colors of late spring. The nagging headache, which always felt to her as if someone were pulling steel wires from her head, was gone now. The lovely view was soothing to her troubled mind.

She remembered that she had been ashamed, as she rode to the steady click of the steel wheels over rail joints, of her actions earlier in the day. At the time, though, it had seemed perfectly plausible for her to drink the mixture she believed to be laudanum and camphor. Her head ached badly, and it occurred to her that if the medicine soothed the pain of neuralgia in her arm, as it did, it must certainly soothe the pain in her head. It had been a foolish thing to do, she told herself now. Robert and her enemies promptly represented to the press that it was a suicide attempt. She was glad, now, that the discerning drugstore clerk had given her a harmless mixture instead of what she had ordered.

Myra Bradwell's pleasant voice interrupted her thoughts, and she turned to greet her friend warmly. Myra said her husband wasn't with her this time. "He's very busy and, as you no doubt have heard, has

brought forth a defensive statement from Dr. Patterson."

Mary said yes, she was just reading it. She picked
up the *Tribune*.

"He is a man, I perceive, who suffers pangs of conscience now," Myra said. "This flood of letters and
the resulting publicity in the papers trouble him
greatly. He says it is not true that he has certified
you to be of sound mind, though, Mary. Yet he ad-
mits that reports in the press about arrangements
being perfected for you to go to Springfield are true."

"Here is his mistake," Mary said grimly. She read
aloud: " 'I am willing to record the opinion that such
is the character of her malady she will not be con-
tent . . . and that the experiment . . . will result only
in giving the coveted opportunity to make extended
rambles, to renew the indulgence of her purchasing
mania and other morbid mental manifestations.' "
She put the newspaper down. "I shall disprove those
statements," Mary said firmly. "And I shall disprove
those statements made at my trial, too. I shall show
the world the kind of restraint of which Dr. Patterson says I am incapable. I shall master these urges to
buy which assail me, and I shall demonstrate ability
to live quietly in one place."

"My dear Mary," Myra said softly, "this wander-
lust which has gripped you since Abraham's death is

perfectly understandable. You seek to escape intolerance. There is no insanity in this."

"Yes, but there are politicians today who do not want the widow of Abraham Lincoln in the public eye. My appearance anywhere bestirs memories of a man whose integrity as a president establishes sharp contrasts when put alongside the reputations of some vandals now in office."

Myra sighed. "How terrible," she said, "to be hated and feared by the Stalwarts, and to be used as an instrument against their perpetuation in office by the other wing. Is there no peace for you?"

"Yes," Mary said thoughtfully, "but I shall not rush it."

Myra obviously had decided to change the subject. "And is everything still all right with you, my dear?" She stared about the room. "It seems pleasant enough."

"Oh, my physical surroundings are nice enough," Mary said. "I am permitted to shop now and then, in Aurora. The food is good. I detest these barred windows, of course, and the attendants are with me constantly. It is the stigma which irritates me most— the desire for vindication. It fairly overwhelms me at times. It is something I must obtain for peace of mind."

"Have the reporters bothered you, my dear?"
Myra looked solicitous.

"Very little." Mary sighed. "They press one so,
you know, but then I suppose that their impatient
searching is but a requirement of their work. They
are gentlemen, really. I fear that I forget myself at
times. I fancy sometimes that I am back in the White
House, you see, and that Abraham is near me. Is it
madness to pretend? Those were happy days, you
see, even though the great war was all about us. I am
just a little old lady, then, pretending that I am with
what used to be. They interrupted my reminiscences
one afternoon, and I fear that I left with them the
impression that I truly believed myself back in Washington."

"They wrote that you keep the curtains drawn and
lighted candles about the room," Myra observed.
"You can understand that such news cannot help but
contribute to the impression which your persecutors
seek to preserve."

Mary sighed again. "How difficult it is," she said,
"for someone quite sane, but suspected of being a
lunatic, to act sane. Every little act is subjected to
strange scrutiny. The bars across my window bother
me, and so I draw the curtains now and then to hide
them from my view. I sit alone, you know. So often

through the years I have done that. And now I sit
alone with living flesh and blood of me near by, in
Chicago, and still I have no sons left to me now. None
at all. Robert is some stranger. My son has gone
away."

"Dear lady," Myra said. She patted Mary's hand.
"I really must rush on. If the train is on time, I must."

"Trains are always on time," Mary Lincoln observed, "when a dear one must leave."

Myra smiled. "I shall send word," she said. "I
intend to see Robert tomorrow. He tells me that he
is coming out here again. Perhaps he will be able to
tell you."

"It would," Mary Lincoln said, "be quite apropos."

"We expect it to be early this month," Myra said.
They exchanged fond farewells, and then Myra Bradwell was gone.

It was early the following afternoon, a clear, bright
September day, that Robert and little Mary Lincoln
came to see Mary Todd Lincoln for the last time at
Bellevue. She was dozing by the window and it startled her, at first, to see the child. Then she struggled
sleepily to her feet and smiled.

"My dear little Mary," she said. "I should have
liked to have a sunny child like you."

Her grandchild lisped a reply, and then Robert's

shadow fell across her, and she erased the gentle smile. Her mouth was set firmly in her smooth, round face. She lifted sober eyes to her only living son.

"Ah, Robert. So you have come again?"

"Yes, Mother. How are you?" The eyes into which she looked were troubled ones.

"I am well, Robert." Mary used the distant, detached tone of voice which came naturally to her now when she spoke with Robert, as with other strangers. Her voice grew warm again. "And how is little Abraham?"

"He is well, thank you." Robert's voice was a sigh. "I have seen the Bradwells. Have they told you?"

Mary said Myra had told her that he would bring word.

Robert sighed again. "The letters have been cruel," he said.

"There is retributive justice in this world, Robert. I have a stain upon me now. Nothing can erase it."

Robert's manner became eager now. "September tenth," he said. "Ninian Edwards will come for you. I shall escort you, too, if you wish."

"Ninian will suffice," she said, and there was a coldness in her voice. "I should prefer only a friend."

She saw the hurt in Robert's face, and it twisted inside her, but she said no more. It was strange, Mary thought at that moment, how much her son's troubled brow looked like Abraham's.

"I have arranged for Amanda to be with you at Springfield," Robert said. "You seem to prefer her of all the . . . the attendants."

Mary said yes, that was true.

"I shall forward checks to Uncle Ninian for your comfort and support, and if you will communicate any other wishes to me, I shall see to them."

Mary ignored this. Instead, she moved to a closet and said, "I have two doll babies here for Mary." Her eyes returned to Mary and lighted again. "You will love them, child. They are so sweet. Almost real, they are. Fine workmanship. Made in Germany, I believe."

She procured the dolls and tucked them into the child's arms.

"Thank you, Grandmama," little Mary said. "They are pretty, Grandmama."

"Little Mary." Mary Lincoln knelt to hug her granddaughter and she felt tears come to her eyes. "Children are a blessing," she said, wondering why she should tell this to a small child. She rose suddenly, and her eyes caught Robert's pained ones. "But they can cause one great pain," she muttered.

They continued to talk as strangers, and Mary told

herself that Robert did not realize the extent of the resentment against him now building within her. She also realized, from his voice and actions, that he thought her quite mad, and yet happier than she had been. If he could only know! she thought. How it would shock this man now strange to me if he were to know!

When Robert and little Mary had gone, Mary Lincoln turned to the ever-present attendant hovering near by. "If you will order my carriage prepared and alert my nurse," she said abruptly, "I should like to go into Aurora tomorrow. I have some final shopping to do."

She saved the gifts she obtained on that shopping trip carefully, keeping them in a closet until Ninian came for her. She told herself, thinking of Dr. Patterson's letter, that she must be careful about such purchases now. This was no indulgence of a purchasing mania, as he called it, but she thought she really ought to give those who had been kind to her at this place some little remembrance. Socks for the men, perfume for the ladies. They would appreciate it.

Ninian was in a jolly mood when he came. He had arranged a private car for her, he said, for the trip to Springfield. The Fox River Valley was a riot of fall colors now. The trip would do her good, and she could rest at Springfield. Robert had remained with the private car at the tracks. Dr. Patterson would join them there.

It pleased Mary to distribute the gifts she had bought. She gave each one to the person for whom she meant it, and some of the ladies had tears in their eyes.

"What about my property?" Mary wanted to know. "There are so many trunks. Trunks here, some in Milwaukee and some at Robert's house, I believe." She stared down at her somber black attire. "My box of jewels, I believe, is at the bank."

Ninian Edwards patted the small hand of his sister-in-law. "Please do not fret about these things, Mary. They will be attended to all in good time."

His presence reassured her. This was no trick of Robert's, she told herself. Not with Ninian here. She spoke briefly to Robert, nodded to Dr. Patterson and seated herself by a window, staring into the distance. Once in Springfield, she thought, there would be many more letters to write. How long would it take, she wondered, to get another trial?

The train lurched and moved forward, and she caught a glimpse of herself reflected in the window. Her face seemed very pale, almost as if chiseled from white marble. Her bluish-gray eyes were large and luminous, and her mouth sad.

She thought, I am returning to the place where Abraham and I were wed. There will be friends about me again.

She blinked her eyes and ceased her meditations. Then she focused them upon the brilliant autumn hues now mottling the Fox River Valley. It had been verdant with spring greens when last she saw it. Now the frosts had come and painted colors across it. It was like life, she thought. She was in her autumn, too. How many years yet? How many? Mary Todd Lincoln felt tired and alone again. She could not mind it when release came, she told herself, but neither would she seek it. She straightened then, and thrust her small chin forward resolutely. But first the trial, the vindication. Then let it come when it would, but not among strangers.

The room on the second floor of her sister's home in Springfield was a pleasant, sunny one. Even during the cold winter months, warm sunlight slanted through the windows, and Mary Lincoln sat there and wrote her letters and dreamed of the day when she might have another trial.

A kind of peace she had not known for years settled over her. Ninian was kind to her, and so was her sister Elizabeth. Frances, her other sister, visited now and then. Mary was always glad to see her, too. That first day, after her arrival, she had seen the

children, passing the house on their way to school.
They had stared curiously at the second-story window, and behind the curtains Mary flinched, wondering what stories these children had been told about
her presence here.

That was why she wanted the curtains drawn, she
told herself. There were no eyes filled with malice
here, but eyes filled with curiosity and pity hurt every
bit as much. And often, therefore, she wrote during
daylight hours by candlelight. A kind of intolerance
which Abraham had fought still lurked in the world
just beyond the windowsill.

The winter months wore on, their passing measured
by the steady scratching of Mary's busy pen. Spring
came and winter's coldness fled, and Mary did not
have the curtains drawn so often now. The long fight,
she told herself, was nearly over. She stared about the
room at her trunks and possessions. Why did she keep
them here, so close about her? She knew the answer
to that question.

They had tried, last year, to take everything from
her. Indeed, they had taken her money and her bonds.
And now she would collect her belongings once again
and have them with her in the twilight of her life.

It had seemed an eternity, really, she told herself,
that June day when Ninian's footsteps sounded on

the stairs. He knocked and she said to come, and his face was creased with a gentle smile as he entered.

"Mary, the arrangements are made."

Her heart leaped. To be free again, really free!

"I have conversed with Mr. Leonard Swett and he is agreeable to our plan. We shall petition for removal of Robert as your conservator and for restoration of all rights, privileges and property. Mr. Swett seems pleased that he is to be granted the privilege of doing you this favor."

"Mr. Swett," Mary said grimly, "is undoing that which he did to me a year ago." She studied Ninian. "Will Robert be there?"

"He need not be," Ninian said.

"Good," Mary said. "I have caused a fury to rage about him, and I do not want it in the courtroom again." She paused. "And Dr. Patterson?"

"Will not be there," Ninian finished for her. "The Bradwell correspondence has quite subdued him."

"When will it be?" she wanted to know.

"This afternoon," Ninian replied. "Blaine failed to get the nomination. Judge Bradwell arranged it immediately. Leonard Swett will be your attorney. It is all arranged."

"As before." She said it as a statement of fact and not as a question.

Ninian smiled. "As before," he said, "but much less painfully. It should be very short."

"It is all arranged then," she said flatly.

"As before," he said, and she detected a kind of joyous sarcasm in his voice.

"And so the Stalwarts have been downed," she mused.

"It will require more than a nomination," Ninian said.

"Yes." Mary grimaced. "They will try to get to the nominee. Who is he?"

"Rutherford B. Hayes," Ninian said. "They say he is a reformer."

"How I stopped them once," Mary said. "How I kept them from their little games! And Abraham did not even know. He trusted them, I suppose. I could understand this. But I stopped them, and they hate me for it yet."

"Yes," Ninian said. "I know, my dear." There was a pause before Ninian went on.

"James and Myra Bradwell are overjoyed. They have turned it for you, Mary."

"I will be free to manage my own affairs," she mused.

"Yes."

"Restored to sanity." Her voice was sarcastic.

"Yes." Ninian's voice was sad.

"Mockery," she said.

"Mockery," he repeated. "But poetic justice, too."

The trip to Chicago, like the winter's waiting, seemed an eternity. Her nose was smudged and she felt sticky, but Mary Lincoln did not mind. The trial came and then was over, lasting only minutes. Ninian was the sole witness. He told the court that her friends all said she was of sound mind and capable of managing her own affairs. "We think she is sane and capable of managing her own property."

"And Robert Lincoln, sir? What is his disposition in this case?"

Judge Wallace had directed his query to Leonard Swett. Mary watched color flow into the burly lawyer's face.

"I had assumed, your honor, that the court had been informed," Swett said. "Mr. Lincoln does not oppose the action. He waives all technicalities."

"The court has been informed, Mr. Swett. The court wanted it in the record." Judge Wallace paused. "And Dr. Patterson?"

"The doctor chooses not to appear," Swett said lamely.

Judge Wallace said he understood. He told the jury it might retire and deliberate, but the foreman said that would not be needed.

"You have a verdict ready, sir?"

"Yes, your honor."

"And what is the verdict?"

The foreman read from a piece of paper: " 'We, the undersigned jurors in the case wherein Mary Lincoln, who was heretofore found to be insane and who is now alleged to be restored to reason, having heard the evidence in said cause, find that the said Mary Lincoln is restored to reason and is capable to manage and control her estate.' "

"Again," Mary Lincoln said, "the rehearsals have been most thorough."

Ninian shushed her. She felt both a fury and a jubilance rise within her. She managed to keep her smooth countenance inscrutable. Only once, during the return trip to Springfield, did she break her self-imposed silence. Ninian turned to her thoughtfully.

"You are very quiet, Mary. Are you not satisfied?"

"I have been thinking, Ninian," she said. "I was arrested, tried, found insane and ordered put away within four hours' time. I came back, was tried, found sane and ordered released in four minutes' time. Can it be now that anyone will doubt that these were political sanity trials?"

"Yes, dear Mary," Ninian said sadly. "There will be doubt and ignorance. Some day, perhaps, the world will know."

"Yes," she said. She studied Ninian. "Rutherford B. Hayes . . . I do not know him. Is he a good man?"

Ninian shrugged. "Time will tell. Robert Ingersoll's plumed knight thinks not."

"He is a prophet," Mary said, "without honor 'neath his visor." She studied for a moment. "And Robert is a little boy lost."

And then Mary Todd Lincoln was silent, deep in thought. She would now write Robert a letter which he would carry seared into his mind and soul to his dying day.

Vengeance is mine, she told herself, and though she knew this was wrongful fury, she vowed to follow it.

Upon arriving back in her room, Mary Todd Lincoln hurriedly procured her pen and paper and commenced to write, but the fury rose in her and choked her, and she left it. For thirteen ugly months, she thought, she had been marked and handled as a lunatic, and this was all because of a weakness in her son. The stain which she now felt would last her life had been dashed on her by men with political motives, and they had betrayed her to her own son.

It was June nineteenth before she could bring herself to write the letter. Yet, she shrieked back at a shrieking conscience, it must be done. Outside, someone snickered and she started. Then she moved to the heavy curtains and drew them closed. The candle wicks stubbornly resisted her efforts to set fire to them, but at last they flickered feebly and then brightened. She adjusted them on the table and sat down slowly, picked up her pen and dipped it thoughtfully. The months of bitterness welled up within her. She put the pen to the paper and began:

Robert T. Lincoln do not fail to send me without the least delay, all my paintings, my silver set and other articles your wife appropriated. . . .

The pen scratched furiously as its user wrote angry, calculated words. She paused at last to study her final remarks, then nodded.

Send me all that I have written for, you have tried your game of robbery long enough. On yesterday, I received two telegrams from prominent Eastern lawyers. You have injured yourself, not me, by your wicked conduct.

Mary told herself that she did not really believe this. Robert had been hurt, but not so much as she.

There was a stain on her now. She was Mary Lincoln, Lunatic.

Mary studied the letter again soberly. She thought of Mary and Abraham, Robert's children, and of Jessie Harlan, who would not be a year old until November. She sighed and thought then to tear the letter to shreds and forget about it, but she could not bring herself to do that. She picked up the pen again, reluctantly, and signed the letter: *Mrs. A. Lincoln.*

Her restlessness increased during the weeks that followed, and she thought more than once to pack up and leave, but the words of Dr. Patterson's *Tribune* letter haunted her. What was it he had written? Oh, yes. About "the coveted opportunity to make extended rambles."

The mark of insanity with which they had stained her was a burning shame on her now as October's chill approached. Warm climates called to her. Where would they be?

Pau, she thought. That was it. Pau, capital of the old province of Béarn, in France. Pau, where the air was clear and warm and soothing, and where the sun shone brightest in the winter months. An ideal resort for nervous persons, she remembered. A place of strangers, too. This, she told herself, was most important of all.

She mentioned it to Elizabeth the following day, and watched the startled look cross her sister's countenance.

"But your friends are about you now, Mary. Would you leave them? And your things are here. All of your things. It seemed to me, dear sister, that Robert gave to you a most scrupulous accounting."

"Yes, Lizzie." Mary sighed and managed a grim little smile. "Including the expenditure of a hundred and fifty-one dollars for hack hire and shadowing by Pinkerton detectives."

"But would you go abroad, Mary? To a land of strangers?"

"There is more tolerance for a Lincoln's widow there than here," Mary said. "I cannot endure to meet my former friends, Lizzie. They will never cease to regard me as a lunatic. I feel it in their soothing manner. If I should say the moon is made of green cheese, they would heartily and smilingly agree with me. I love you, but I cannot stay. I would be much less unhappy in the midst of strangers."

Mary watched disappointment flood her sister's eyes, and then surrender. Lizzie, Mary decided, would not argue the matter further.

"And will you write again to Robert, Mary? Your last letter to him has caused him great grief."

"I know no Robert," Mary Lincoln said. "There were three sons and they are taken from me now. I do not know this Robert. Who is Robert?"

And Mary Lincoln turned from her sister and mounted the stairs to her room.

Chapter 8

BUNDLED IN A BLANKET, Mary Todd Lincoln sat
quietly in the deck chair and watched the New York
skyline loom ever larger on the reeling horizon beyond
the steamer *Amérique's* bow.

The sun was warm on her face, but the sea breeze
was chilly. It seemed to pierce the heavy robe in
which the ship's nurse had wrapped her. She shifted
uncomfortably, feeling the fiery flash of pain streak
up her back. She lay back wearily, reflecting how
very tired she was these days. If only she hadn't
fallen off that stepladder back in Pau, she reflected,
she might have made it. She might have lived out her
remaining years among those strangers whose very
ignorance of her true identity had been as a shield
about her.

These had been lonely years, she thought, with not

one familiar face in them. And yet they had been the happiest ones she had spent since Abraham was shot down. There was, she decided, a great deal to be said for solitude. Mary sighed as she turned her mind to Robert. She could not forgive him, nor Swett, nor the others. Not even now, when it no longer mattered. Robert was successful in his way. A good lawyer, they said, and a good cabinet member. Mary thought about that.

Mary turned her mind back to herself; there was decidedly something wrong. The constant thirst, the boils, the loss of weight and the failing sight; the palsied hands, the great weariness and the sudden onslaught of age marks long held back, which had brought white to her hair and deep lines about her eyes and mouth. She watched the ship's nurse approach, balancing a glass of water on a small tray. The nurse smiled and bent low, so that she might take the glass. She hesitated and then raised the glass precariously to her lips to drink deeply, and when she had finished, she breathed hard and then drank again. At last she put the emptied glass back on the tray.

"I have such a thirst," she said simply. "It is with me all the time." The nurse's pleasant features were blurred and Mary squinted to focus her eyes.

"Water is good for madame," the nurse said. Mary

wondered if this nurse knew her true identity. She doubted it. She had managed to keep the secret for so long that she had become expert at it. Robert, her only living son, had made her a stranger, she thought. She could not bear the label he had fastened to her: Mary Lincoln, Lunatic.

"I crave water so," she said. "It is one of many torments. My back, the boils and the constant running waters." She felt a slight flush warm her cheeks and wondered if it was indelicate to speak of it this way. She decided not. This was a nurse. "It is most inconvenient," she finished lamely.

The nurse's eyes were kind. Mary Lincoln thought of Beatrice. She had the same sort of eyes.

"Are you comfortable, madame? Perhaps a little stroll?"

Mary said no, she was much too tired for that. Perhaps it was the air. "It has helped my appetite, but I continue to lose weight. I am below one hundred pounds now."

"Then you must conserve your strength, madame, for the docking. It will be soon now. Are you all packed and ready?"

Mary said yes, thank you, her baggage arrangements had all been made. "Will it be soon now? I am very anxious to set foot ashore again."

She wasn't really, she told herself. She was not anxious to set foot on American soil at all. There was a stigma lurking here which attached to her. There was a stain on her here which nothing could erase now. Not even death. Her first-born had seen to that.

Mary squirmed beneath the blanket again and found a position in which the gnawing spinal pain seemed not so great. She thought that perhaps she ought to go directly to Dr. Lewis A. Sayre in New York. He was the leading orthopedic surgeon of his time. He could determine quickly if this great weariness stemmed from her fall. She remembered, then, that some had branded her insane because of her previous complaints about this other illness which had grown with the years. She decided against going to Dr. Sayre immediately. She would go back to Springfield, instead, and try to rest there. If her symptoms grew worse, then she could come back here.

"Have you been abroad long, madame?" The nurse's voice thrust itself into her thoughts.

"Four years," Mary said. "That is, it will be four years in October. But this is October, isn't it?"

The nurse said yes. "The first. My! You have been away for a long time."

Mary Lincoln sighed tiredly. October 1, 1880. "I

spent most of the time in Pau, living in a small apartment," she said. "I would be there yet had it not been for the fall."

"The fall, madame?" The nurse looked interested and Mary remembered that she had not told her about that.

"It was such an irony," Mary said, and in spite of herself, she smiled faintly. "Lace curtains have been my downfall before."

"Lace curtains?"

"Yes. They were hanging crooked, you see. I could never stand to see such curtains hanging crooked, and so I fetched a ladder and climbed up to adjust them. It was then I fell. It was painful. Very painful. I was in bed for weeks."

Mary was thinking that Dr. Patterson could never accuse her now of living in any manner but an unpretentious one. She had lived alone in the small apartment, spending most of her time there. There had been little prodding by the curious except for that one time when a tourist from America thought he recognized her and told others of it. That was in April of 1877, she remembered. This, coupled with the fact that the weather was getting colder at Pau and the boils were bothering her again, had sent her on a trip to Marseilles and Naples and Sorrento. The warm sunshine seemed to help more than anything else. But in the end she had returned to Pau. After all, it was the most noted health resort in all of Europe, and they said the Vichy water would be good for her.

She grinned at that. The Vichy water had not helped one bit as far as she was concerned.

"Is the pain of that fall still with you, madame? Is that why you walk so slowly and so uncertainly?"

Mary said that was a great part of it. "The weakness is the rest. Sometimes when I am on my feet I feel faint and weary and I must take hold of something to steady myself. It was not the fall alone. It has been many things, many things through the years."

"It will be good for you to get home again, madame. It is good to be with friends and family. You have a family, of course?"

Mary told the nurse about her sisters and her grandnephew, Lewis Baker, Jr., but she did not mention Robert. She thought again of her first-born son and sighed. She had not communicated with him in all this time. Maternal love and pride had only once pierced the cold barrier which had risen between them—when she read in a Parisian newspaper that he was being mentioned as a possible presidential candidate. She had derived a grim sort of pleasure out of that. Robert would never make it, she told herself. Not now. Politicians had seen to that at her expense.

Mary told herself that her son did possess some good qualities, but they were not those which had marked Abraham as a man apart. Abraham, she thought grimly, had been kind, even to his step-mother.

Mary had not forgotten Robert's children, though. This was particularly true of her little namesake Mary. She wondered why they had nicknamed the child Mamie. Through Lewis Baker she had sent many small presents to the child. She turned her mind back to Robert and felt the old bitterness well up within her. God forgive her! She could not bring herself to turn the other cheek. Not even to her own flesh and blood. She sighed and decided that she was not at all like Abraham in such matters. No. Not at all. She was just not like her husband. She could never forgive Robert for what he had done.

A young couple walked by, conversing animatedly and pointing to the rising skyline of the great city just ahead, and both turned curious faces toward her. She lowered her eyes and averted her face. It was curious, she thought, how she seemed to shrink away from the outside world now. She decided she was tired of faces. All faces. She found a certain ironic humor in this. There had been years when she wanted

everyone to see her. The whole world. Now she did
not particularly care to see anyone. Not anyone.

"I will be most happy," she muttered, "when I am
with Abraham again."

"Oh? Is Abraham a son?"

"My husband," Mary said.

"And you have been away from him four years?"
The nurse looked puzzled.

"No. Fifteen years," Mary said. "Abraham is
dead."

"I wondered if you were married," the nurse said,
"and then I saw the ring."

"Ah yes, the ring." Mary studied it, and removed
it. It was very worn now, she thought. "It is Etrus-
can gold," she said simply. "I have had it many,
many years." Her eyes studied the inscription and
though it seemed blurred to her, she knew what it
said: *A. L. to Mary, Nov. 4, 1842. Love is Eternal.*
"It is quite old," she said. "Thirty-eight years next
month, as a matter of fact."

"Thirty-eight years?" The nurse looked aston-
ished.

"Yes, my dear. More years than are upon you, I
venture." She managed a faint smile. "Yes, I
daresay."

"And your husband has been gone for fifteen
years," the nurse said slowly. "I am sorry, madame."

Mary felt the old anguish which always seemed so fresh and new drive itself through her again. Pain flamed up her spine and her vision blurred even more. The crushing weariness seemed to make her sag inside.

"Yes, fifteen years. The war . . ."

"Oh. The Civil War?" The nurse looked sad. "Yes, they say it took so many. That has been some time now. I was a very little girl then."

"Sometimes," Mary said tiredly, "it seems like an eternity, but then I can stand an eternity, you see. Our love was eternal. It is eternal."

The young woman's eyes probed into hers now and they softened. "It is good to know, madame, that such love exists." She looked thoughtful and said, "Fifteen years . . . I thought that the war was over then?"

"No," Mary said. "Sometimes I think it was only just beginning then."

The nurse was studying her intently now and Mary wondered what she thought. She remembered the scrutiny she had given herself before the mirror this morning when she had her new spectacles on. The fat of middle age was gone, but her face seemed haggard and drawn and the streaks of white through her hair added to the impression of great age. Her clothing was ill fitting now because of her loss of weight. Her hand sought out the outline of the mourning brooch at her bosom.

"Only this remains unchanged," she said, and she perceived that the nurse did not understand her remark.

The bawling of deck hands interrupted them. The nurse rose to her feet. "We are headed into the slip now," she said. "Will you want to go back to your stateroom, madame?"

Mary said yes, to straighten up and to pick up a few personal things. The nurse helped her to her feet and took her there.

Inside, she sat tiredly fussing with her hair and then her bonnet. At last she rose and slipped into her heavy coat. It must be rather warm in New York for October, she thought, but there was a chill inside her which she could not warm. The heavy coat would be best. She pulled the coat about her frail figure and walked uncertainly and with a noticeable limp to the door.

The nurse was waiting for her, smiling. "I thought that perhaps madame might like for me to escort her down the gangplank," she explained. "It is rather treacherous even when one has the best of footing."

"No," Mary decided firmly. "No, thank you,

young lady. Do not misunderstand me please. I appreciate your kindness and attention. It is just that I must walk by myself here. What awaits me ashore I do not seek to thrust on anyone."

There were times when the pain was not so bad, she thought, but at those times the partial paralysis of her legs seemed worse. And now the pain was not so bad, but the deck seemed to writhe below her and the footing was uncertain. She stared down the slope of the gangplank, thrust one foot forward tentatively, and then began descending.

As Mary Lincoln groped her way ashore, holding desperately to the handrail, she heard loud cheering and turned startled eyes to the milling throng below and ahead of her. The hundreds of faces were blurred, so that she could not make out the features on any one of them, and yet they all seemed to be turned toward her. She thought of turning back and seeking out the ship's nurse, and then, for a fleeting moment, the old lure called out to her, the old love of being seen and greeted by the many. She took a firmer grip upon the handrail, set her generous mouth firmly in a straight, determined line and moved on.

The cheering and the cries of greeting grew louder now. Mary Lincoln felt a flush of pride rise in her cheeks, experienced a gnawing hope. Could this be

for her? Yes, she told herself. It could be. Had not
she wired Elizabeth her intentions? Someone would
have come to meet her and take her to Springfield.

It must have got into the papers then! Yes, that
would be it. The newspapers. She was forgiven, and
not forgotten. The stain was gone. They were her
friends again. All of them. After all, she was the
widow of Abraham Lincoln.

She reached the bottom of the gangplank and almost fell, staggering awkwardly as her feet hit the
pavement. Her back had commenced to throb again,
but she felt the flush of the old excitement in her
cheeks. It was an effort to walk this way, but she held
herself proudly erect.

The first snickers of amusement stunned and then
terrified her. She halted uncertainly, seeking to focus
her eyes on the hundreds of faces. She wished she had
put on her spectacles now. Someone near by laughed
and raised a hand to jab a pointing finger at her. She
drew back, feeling a sudden great emptiness inside of
her. It was then that she saw the policeman moving
swiftly toward her.

She flinched as he placed a heavy hand on her
shoulder, and thought of that time in her hotel room
in Chicago when Leonard Swett had placed her under arrest.

"Back with ye now," the officer was saying. "Back now, me woman. Make way here."

Mary Lincoln felt the strong arm in blue sweep her aside. She stumbled clear, teetered and regained her balance. Then she turned curious eyes to watch. A beautiful woman—quite overdressed, she thought— swept by toward a waiting carriage. Other women followed. People were calling out and throwing kisses. Mary Lincoln squinted with the effort to focus her eyes, but the lady's face remained blurred. From the noises of the crowd, though, she knew that this must be someone of prominence.

Her curiosity overwhelmed her at last.

"Who was it, sir?" she inquired of a man next to her.

She watched surprise cross his face. "You mean to say, madame, that you did not recognize Madam Sarah Bernhardt?"

Mary shook her head no and managed a sheepish look.

"The first lady of the footlights!" the man said admiringly.

A first lady? Mary Todd Lincoln turned away slowly and saw then the familiar face of Lewis Baker. As he came to her, she sobbed and put her head on his chest, feeling the great weariness within her.

"There, there, Auntie Mary," Lewis was saying. "I'm sorry I was late. I have the carriage waiting."

"It is all right, Lewis," Mary Lincoln said at last. "All right. Let us go quickly please. I have seen a first lady just now, but there is no fascination in me for first ladies any more."

Chapter 9

"IT IS A fierce monotony filled with pain and pungent grief," Mary said slowly. She moved haltingly across the room. Bright sunlight streamed in through open windows. "God alone can ease my burden, Lizzie, until I am reunited with my dearly beloved husband and my children."

Mary Lincoln turned, with some effort, to face her sister, and saw the torment in Lizzie's eyes.

"Do not grieve, dear Lizzie," she said. She felt her mind rise then and soar to distant heights as it often did when she thought of Abraham. "He walked among them as a prince," she said. "Nothing they have done or can do will ever change that now. Only my return to him will assuage this sorrow which has been about me these many years like a clinging mantle."

"You walk much better today, Mary," Lizzie said, and Mary heard the attempt at cheerfulness in her sister's voice. "This long period abed is what has made you melancholy. I do believe you are improving rapidly now."

"The boils are so troublesome to me." Mary sighed. "And my hands—see how swollen they are?" She moved painfully to the small table near the bed. "I must remove the ring until the swelling goes down." She tugged at the worn gold band and felt weak for the effort of it. It gave at last and she slipped it off, peering at it, and then she placed it on the table. It saddened her that she must do this.

"It is warm," Lizzie said. "Very warm. This has been such a hot, dry summer. Is there anything which would make you more comfortable?"

"Perhaps a glass of water, Lizzie. I have such a thirst."

"Why, of course, dear Mary." Mary listened to the sounds of Lizzie descending the stairs. Then she stared at the small calendar at her small writing desk. July 14, 1882.

"My Gethsemane is ever with me, dear Lord," she said. "When will it be over? Oh, when?"

She had lasted it out for one year here on the hill at Springfield and then decided on one last attempt to ease the pain wracking her weary frame. Dr. Sayre in New York had been very kind, as she remembered him when they were friends in Lexington. He told her frankly that the inflammation of her spinal cord, resulting from the fall at Pau, had partially paralyzed the lower part of her body. He said it would get worse, and that her entire body might be paralyzed one day. She had written some friends about it, but had elected not to tell Lizzie. Lizzie had enough worries as it was.

She found, at the Clarendon Hotel, where she stayed, that she was becoming increasingly unable to walk without the aid of a chair. Even using a chair, she was likely to fall at times. It was a persecution of a sort, she thought, but then her life was filled with persecutions. Another one made little difference really. After all, she was only waiting.

She held Robert at a distance from her still, and yet, she told herself grudgingly, she was proud of him. They were saying he was a good cabinet officer. She told herself grimly that there must be some ironic justice in Robert's presence at the shooting of poor James Garfield. Robert was traveling about a great deal now with President Arthur. He and his daughter Mary had visited her every two or three weeks at the hotel in New York, and later at the Turkish, Electric and Roman Baths operated by Dr. Miller.

Mary sighed. None of the treatments seemed to help. And as the cold, wet March days passed and the first blush of the spring of 1882 was yet a promise in the air, she had returned to her sister's home. And she thought, as she rode the rails back to Springfield that time, that this might be the last of it.

It mattered little to her that in January of this year Congress had increased her pension to five thousand dollars a year. It had been important to her, earlier, though, when the matter of Garfield's widow and Grant's need of money came before the House and Senate. At least, it had seemed important. Was she not in direst poverty?

Mary sighed. She had found it increasingly difficult, through these years, to draw a line of distinction between poverty of pocketbook and poverty of affection. Perhaps she ought to have tried more strenuously to do so. She listened to Lizzie climbing the stairs and reached eagerly for the glass of water. She drank deeply, thanked her sister and sat down tiredly.

"It has been nearly forty years," he said thoughtfully. "Nearly forty years, Lizzie, since my feet crossed the threshold of this house as a bride. That is a long, long time, isn't it?"

Lizzie said yes, it was, but it would be best not to think about it now.

"But I dwell in the past, Lizzie. It is a fancy of mine. The past is all I have, you see. There is no afterglow to it. It is all what was and what might have been."

"I understand, my dear, but you must think of yourself now."

"*Ich dien,*" Mary said in German. "I serve. I serve a memory as best I can, and so I have for seventeen years now. Before that, God knows, I walked beside him doing those things which I felt to be best for him. If I erred in judgment, God forgive me."

"There was no error, dear sister."

"Yes. Perhaps. I fancy sometimes lately that I can see errors now. But I was young and beautiful once. They said that. Even those who spoke ill of me and gossiped about me said that. And I was ambitious, too, for my dearly beloved."

"Do not think of the past, Mary."

"I do not know why they whispered so. Washington is a place filled with animosities and cruel gossip though. It is a carnivorous society there which feeds on the meat of the gentle ones."

"You must rest, Mary."

"My rest is near at hand."

"You must not speak like this. Ah, Mary, you speak of it so often these days. It is the heat."

"No, not the heat. I do not mind those things which nature does to me. It has been what people have done which yet afflicts me."

"I am driving out tomorrow, Mary. Perhaps you would like to go with me again?"

"I should only just sit there, in the closed carriage outside the store, and people would stare and point and speak about me in hushed tones. Or perhaps I would purchase some dressgoods, knowing all the while that those about me would speak, after my departure, of my trunks of unused goods. It is a certain knowledge that is cruelty too."

Lizzie sighed. "As you wish, Mary."

"Have I been such a great burden to you, Lizzie? I know I have. You and Ninian have been so kind."

"No burden, dear Mary. What little we have done we owe to mankind and to you. We love you, dear sister. We love you very much."

It comforted her. Mary told herself she needed love. She needed all the love she could get. The familiar numbness played about her knees and hips now, and she rose and made her way to the bed.

"I shall rest awhile," she said. Lizzie nodded, biting her lip, and tiptoed from the room. And Mary Todd Lincoln lay back to watch happier moments of her life pass before her.

She had only just dozed, she told herself, looking up into Lizzie's anxious countenance. But Lizzie said not, it was Saturday now, and Mary had not even roused when they treated her boils. She must try to eat something.

Mary said she would, watching astonishment spread across her sister's face. She asked what was the matter? Lizzie had tears in her eyes. She turned away, and Mary realized, with a start, that no sounds were issuing from her mouth.

Lizzie and the doctor came and went away again, during the day, and once Ninian came to her and looked into her eyes and held her hand.

Night fell and they came with lamps. The paralysis gripped her with iron claws now. The pain was fading. She could no longer feel the dull, drawing hurt of the boils. She wished that they would turn up the light.

She heard them say once that it was daylight now and someone—her vision was so blurred she knew not who—came and took the lamps away. They could not fool her, she thought, grinning to herself. It was night and they wanted her to rest. She closed her eyes tiredly and the grip of the paralysis seemed to loosen a bit. The blackness came then, swirling about her, and yet, she thought, she could not sleep.

Once, she knew that Dr. Dresser was in the room

again. She heard him speaking with Lizzie and heard her sobbing. And then it was very quiet for a long time.

She felt and heard the fresh breeze as it rustled the curtains and blew into the room. She was glad. There was a scent of rain about it. It had been so dry and hot that a fresh rain would be good.

Mary Lincoln tried to move but failed. The paralysis was complete now, she thought. Then the darkness came again, and this time, with it, a voice. It rather startled her at first—perhaps because she had not heard the softness of it for so many years. What was it saying? She strained to hear.

It was a soft, compelling voice, filled with sympathy and with love. And it was saying, as no other voice quite like it ever could say: "Come, Mary dear. Come to me. Your trial is ended now."

Mary found she could move then. She reached first for the worn gold ring and was surprised to find that it went so easily onto the swollen finger.

"Love is eternal," she said.

Then Mary Lincoln rose from her bed and went to the voice.

BIBLIOGRAPHY
AND
INDEX

Bibliography

Abraham Lincoln Quarterly. Published by Abraham Lincoln Association, Springfield, Ill. Issues of March 1945, Dec. 1945, Dec. 1947, Sept. 1949, March 1950.

ANGLE, PAUL M. ed. *The Lincoln Reader.* New Brunswick, N. J., 1947.

BARTON, WILLIAM E. *The Life of Abraham Lincoln.* 2 vols. Indianapolis, 1925.

———. *The Women Lincoln Loved.* Indianapolis, 1927.

BAYNE, JULIA TAFT. *Tad Lincoln's Father.* Boston, 1931.

BURGESS, JOHN W. *The Administration of President Hayes.* New York, 1916.

CARPENTER, FRANCIS B. *The Inner Life of Abraham Lincoln: Six Months at the White House.* Boston, 1883.

COLVER, ANNE. *Mr. Lincoln's Wife.* New York, 1943.

EVANS, W. A., M.D. *Mrs. Abraham Lincoln: A Study of Her Personality and Influence on Lincoln.* New York, 1932.

The First Year of American Heritage, Dec. 1954-1955. Issue of Aug. 1955, p. 10.

GERNON, BLAINE BROOKS. *The Lincolns in Chicago.* Chicago, 1934.

GOLTZ, CARLOS W. *Incidents in the Life of Mary Todd Lincoln.* Sioux City, Iowa, 1928.

Grimsley, Elizabeth Todd. "Six Months in the White House," *Journal of the Illinois State Historical Society,* Oct. 1926-Jan. 1927, pp. 43-63.

Glyndon, Howard. "The Truth About Mrs. Lincoln," *The Independent,* Aug. 10, 1882.

Helm, Katherine. *The True Story of Mary, Wife of Lincoln.* New York, 1928.

Herndon, William H. *A Letter to Isaac N. Arnold.* Library of Congress, privately printed, 1938.

———, and Weik, Jesse W. *Herndon's Life of Lincoln.* New York, 1889 and 1902.

Herr, John. *In Defense of the Lincoln Family.* Cynthiana, Ky., 1943.

Holden, Walter S. *Abraham Lincoln, A Man of Inner Conflict.* Toronto, 1944.

Journal of the Illinois State Historical Society, Vol. XXXI, No. 3 (Sept. 1938). Springfield, Ill.

Keckley, Elizabeth. *Behind the Scenes.* New York, 1868.

Kent, C. William. "Lincoln and Davis," *Third Annual Report of the Ohio Valley Historical Association,* Vol. III (1910), 51-61.

Kinnaird, Virginia. "Mrs. Lincoln as a White House Hostess," *Papers in Illinois Historical Society,* 1938.

Lamon, Ward Hill. *The Life of Abraham Lincoln; From His Birth to His Inauguration as President.* Boston, 1872. Ghostwritten by Chauncey F. Black.

Lorant, Stefan. *A Picture of His Life; Books and Articles.* New York, 1957.

Mearns, David C. *The Lincoln Papers: The Story of the Collection with Selections to July 4, 1861.* 2 vols. New York, 1948.

Moos, Malcolm. *The Republicans.* New York, 1956.

Newton, Joseph F. *Lincoln and Herndon.* Cedar Rapids, Iowa, 1910.

NICOLAY, HELEN. *Personal Traits of Abraham Lincoln.* New York, 1912.

NICOLAY, JOHN G., AND HAY, JOHN. *Abraham Lincoln: A History.* New York, 1917.

Official Proceedings of the Republican National Conventions of 1868–1880. Charles W. Johnson, publisher, Minneapolis, 1903.

Papers in Illinois Historical Society, 1938, and *Transcript for the Year 1938.* Illinois State Historical Society, 1939.

RANDALL, RUTH PAINTER. *Mary Lincoln, Biography of a Marriage.* Boston, 1953.

———. *Lincoln's Sons.* Boston, 1955.

SANDBURG, CARL, AND ANGLE, PAUL M. *Mary Lincoln, Wife and Widow.* New York, 1932.

STODDARD, WILLIAM O. *Inside the White House in War Times.* New York, 1890.

TOWNSEND, WILLIAM HENRY. *Lincoln and His Wife's Home Town.* Indianapolis, 1929.

———. *Lincoln and the Blue Grass.* Lexington, Ky., 1955.

Transactions of the Illinois State Historical Society. Publication of the Illinois State Historical Society. Nos. 37, 38, 39.

WALLACE, MRS. FRANCES (TODD). *Lincoln's Marriage.* Newspaper interview, Springfield, Ill., Sept. 2, 1895. Privately printed, 1917.

WARREN, LOUIS A., ed. *Lincoln Lore.* Periodical published by The Lincoln National Life Foundation, Fort Wayne, Indiana. No. 155 (March 28, 1932), No. 193 (Dec. 19, 1932), No. 410 (Feb. 15, 1937), No. 1067 (Sept. 19, 1949), No. 1124 (Oct. 23, 1950), No. 1264 (June 29, 1953).

WHITNEY, MAJ. HENRY C. *Life on the Circuit with Lincoln.* Boston, 1892.

WILLIAMS, CHARLES RICHARD. *Diary and Letters of Rutherford B. Hayes.* Vols. 3 and 7, Hayes Series. Columbus, Ohio, 1922, 1925.

————. *The Life of Rutherford B. Hayes.* Considered vols. 1 and 2, Hayes Series. Boston, 1914.

WILSON, RUFUS ROCKWELL, ed. *Intimate Memories of Lincoln.* Elmira, N. Y., 1945.

Manuscript Collections:

COCHRAN, WILLIAM C. Letter to his mother, June 16, 1876— Re: Republican Convention 1876. Hayes Memorial Library, Fremont, Ohio.

DAVIS, DAVID. MSS. Photostat of Leonard Swett's letter concerning the Sanity Trial of Mrs. Lincoln. Chicago Historical Society.

HAYES, RUTHERFORD B. Campaign material—1876 Convention. Hayes Memorial Library, Fremont, Ohio.

————. Personal Papers—1849–1892. Ohio Historical Library, Columbus, Ohio.

HERNDON-WEIK MSS. Library of Congress.

Illinois State Historical Library Collections. Miscellaneous material.

Lincoln National Life Foundation Collection. Fort Wayne, Indiana (Publisher of *Lincoln Lore*). Dr. R. Gerald McMurtry, director.

Lincoln Administration Papers. Original records of Robert T. Lincoln as conservator of his mother's property while she was under judgment of insanity. Illinois State Historical Library.

LINCOLN. Original Estate Papers of Abraham, Mary Todd, and Thomas Lincoln. Probate Judge's Office, Sangamon County, Springfield, Ill.

LINCOLN, MARY TODD. Court Records of Sanity Trial of, photostats. Illinois State Historical Library.

LINCOLN, ROBERT TODD. Papers of Abraham Lincoln. MSS. Library of Congress.

LINCOLN, THOMAS "TAD." Guardianship, Papers of, photostats.
Probate Judge's Office, Sangamon County, Springfield, Ill.
NICOLAY, J. G. MSS. Library of Congress.

Newspapers:

Aurora, Illinois, *Beacon-News.* Dec. 11, Dec. 25, 1932; Jan. 1,
Jan. 8, 1933.
Chicago *Post and Mail.* July 13, 1875.
Chicago *Tribune.* May 20, May 21, Aug. 8, 1875.

Index

197